I0666598

ONE
LAST
DREAM

A SCREENPLAY

W. E. GUTMAN

CCB Publishing
British Columbia, Canada

One Last Dream: A Screenplay

Copyright ©2012 by W. E. Gutman
ISBN-13   978-1-77143-023-4
First Edition

Library and Archives Canada Cataloguing in Publication
Gutman, W. E., 1937-
One last dream : a screenplay / written by W. E. Gutman.
ISBN 978-1-77143-023-4
Also available in electronic format.
Additional cataloguing data available from Library and Archives
Canada

Adapted by the author for the screen or stage from
his novel *NOCTURNES -- Tales from the Dreamtime* ©2006,
W. E. Gutman.

Screenplay registered 2010 with the Writers' Guild
of America.

Cover design by the author. Eye inset: Operation Cas-
tle/Bravo, 1954, U.S. Atomic Energy Commission.

This book is printed on acid-free paper.

References to real persons, alive or deceased, and allu-
sions to events, factual or contrived, are intended to
lend epic realism to a largely fictionalized account of
personal experiences, insights and meditations.

Publisher: CCB Publishing
              British Columbia, Canada
              www.ccbpublishing.com

TO MY SON TOMMY

Also by W. E. GUTMAN

JOURNEY TO XIBALBA -- The Subversion of Human Rights in Central America © 2000. Reporter's Notebook (out of print).

NOCTURNES -- Tales from the Dreamtime © 2006. Fiction.

FLIGHT FROM EIN SOF © 2009. Fiction.

THE INVENTOR © 2009. Historical fiction.

A PALER SHADE OF RED: Memoirs of a Radical. © 2012. Autobiography.

ONE NIGHT IN COPÁN -- Chronicles of Madness Foretold. Tales of mystery, fantasy and horror. © 2012.

UN DERNIER RÊVE. **(ONE LAST DREAM)** Screenplay (French-language version; translated by the author). © 2012.

People always talk about the
public interest, but all they
really care about is themselves
and private property.

Utopia, Thomas More (1478-1535)

S Y N O P S I S

Dreams are at best impenetrable and mercurial, like droplets of quicksilver. They evoke abstract, warped landscapes. They spawn grotesque characters, hatch aberrant scenarios and force dreamers into absurd, often embarrassing situations. Dreams stalk and hijack unwary sleepers, lay bare their most secret longings and unmask their obsessions and phobias. For all their quirks, false leads, dead ends and truncated climaxes, dreams are the portals to the soul. Could they one day be called upon to trap and subdue wayward dreamers? Isn't the clash of dreams the source of all human discord? Aren't latter-day witch hunts targeting freethinkers, mavericks and dissenters who must be neutralized or silenced if special interests are to maintain their imperial grip on society?

DRAMATIS PERSONAE

JEREMIAH: dream chronicler, agitator

TITUS: dream licensing officer

GRAND OMNIPOTENT DREAMER (GOD): power behind the nightmares

MAGISTRATE: presiding inquisitor

LANGFORD T. HUNNICUT: police inspector

MAN IN OFFICE

EMILE ROUSSEAU: vagrant/dream raider

VAN AKEN: artist

GROUNDSKEEPER

TV ANCHORS, NEWSCASTERS

BAILLIF

EXTRAS

INCIDENTAL MUSIC

Alban Berg: Violin Concerto, 1st movement.

Claude Debussy: Nocturnes; String Quartet; Fantasy for Piano & Orch., part 2.

Gabriel Fauré: Requiem Opus 48, part 1.

Philip Glass: Violin Concerto.

Charles Kœchlin: Les Heures Persanes, parts 14, 15.

Silvestre Revueltas: Night of the Maya, part 4.

Eric Satie: Trois Gymnopédies, Avant-dernières pensées.

Arnold Schoenberg: Verklärte Nacht, parts 1, 2, 3.

Dmitri Shostakovich: Symphony No. 5, parts 3, 4.

Igor Stravinsky: The Rite of Spring, parts 1, 2, 14.

Anton Webern: Five Movements for String Quartet, Op.5.

Kurt Weil: Symphony No. 2; Concerto for Violin and Wind Orchestra.

Fade in to silent footage of war, nuclear mushrooms, urban riots, public executions, insane asylum mayhem, Depression-era bread-lines, manic Hitler speeches, concentration camp charnels, McCarthy-era hearings, Cambodia's killing fields, Charlie Chaplin entangled in giant moving gears (Modern Times), the collapse of New York's Twin Towers, photos of abuse and humiliation at Abu Ghraib and Guantanamo Bay detention centers, imams calling Muslims to devotions from the top of minarets, police brutality, Orthodox Jews praying ecstatically at Jerusalem's Western Wall, frenzied evangelical church "revivals," papal opulence and pageantry, the killing of baby seals, mob violence, etc.

> **JEREMIAH** (voice-over) wearily
>
> Night is neither longer nor shorter
>
> than it's ever been. But it's infi-
>
> nitely darker, too dark to make out
>
> the avatars of man's most hideous
>
> fears. Fear of the unknown. Fear of
>
> change. Fear of reality. Fear of
>
> truth. The horror resumes in the full
>
> blaze of day.

Fade out

Interior. Night. Camera pans from a star-studded sky to a Manhattan high-rise apartment building then, through a window, to a living room. Framed reproductions of Hieronymus Bosch's, Breughel's, Grunewald's and Durer's most bizarre paintings adorn the walls. **Jeremiah** is at his desk, lost in thought, perusing a notebook. He gets up, walks to the window and gazes at New York's diamond-studded nighttime skyline. **Claude Debussy'**s *Nocturnes* No. 1 plays softly in the background.

                    JEREMIAH (voice-over)

Where do I begin? *How* do I begin? I died today -- or was it yesterday? I saw no white lights, no angels. I felt no rapture. All I remember is that I was at the zenith of a career that fed my illusions but kept me hungry and lean. *"Dream or perish,"* they say. I'd stopped marking time. I knew that nothing ever changes. Not the lies, the arrogance, the egotism of the ruling classes; not the vul- garity, the hypocrisy, the restless apathy of the common man. I was tired. Who knows how many more for- bidden dreams I might have spun had I not been silenced by a firestorm that descended from the sky and stilled the earth. But I'm digressing.

Fade out.

Exterior. The **Dream Licensing Bureau (DLB)**, a large windowless hangar-like building. Inside, projected on the eastern wall, a 50-foot holo- graphic likeness of the **Grand Omnipotent Dream-**

er (GOD) smiles with studied remoteness at the hundreds of workers below. File cabinets line the entire perimeter from concrete floor to Olympian ceiling. Everywhere, black-booted clerks wearing canary yellow jumpers scurry up and down mechanized ladders like crazed bees, retrieving or storing documents. As far as the eye can see, row after endless row, licensing officers sit at their desks, sorting out applications, processing requisitions, handing out dispensations or levying fines.

LOUDSPEAKER

Jeremiah, Dream Identification Number 3579. Proceed to Station G, Aisle 27, Desk 937.

Interior. DLB Office. Cultivating an air of bureaucratic nonchalance, Case Officer **Titus** leafs through manuals, sheaves of codes and precedent-setting rulings, each neatly logged under its own acronym. A balding little man with porcine features and pudgy, manicured fingers, he does things by the book.

TITUS

Name, age, dream identification number.

JEREMIAH

Jeremiah. Seventy-five. Three-five-seven-nine.

TITUS

Military status?

JEREMIAH

Honorable separation. Sea Corps. They asked me if I could swim, so I said, 'Why, don't you have ships?'

TITUS

I'm not amused. Hobbies?

JEREMIAH

Yes.

TITUS

Well?

JEREMIAH

I dream. You already know that.

Titus stares at **Jeremiah,** one bushy eyebrow flexed in an all-knowing arc over smudged bifocals.

TITUS

There are dreams and there are *dreams*. When did you start dreaming?

JEREMIAH

As soon as I spurted out of my mother's womb, head first. I was nearly suffocated, blinded. I was cold. I felt vulnerable in my nudity. I was hungry, thirsty. We eat so we can feel hungry again.

TITUS

What do you dream about?

JEREMIAH, feinting modesty

Oh, this and that.

TITUS

Come now, you've got do better. I need a definition. For the record.

JEREMIAH

A definition? Define negative gravity, absolute vacuum, antimatter, infinity. Define a dream.

TITUS

We'll skip that for now. What else do you do?

JEREMIAH

I fly. What's it to you?

TITUS

I ask the questions. What do you fly?

JEREMIAH

A heavier-than-air flying machine.

TITUS

And where does it take you?

JEREMIAH

Where I tell it to. Here and there.

TITUS

Be specific.

JEREMIAH

There's more to flying than filing a flight plan. Is there a law against going around in circles?

TITUS

You've got to land sometime, don't you?

JEREMIAH

Yeah; to refuel.

TITUS

Let's try this again, shall we? Tell me more about your ... aerial excursions.

JEREMIAH

When I was a little boy I had a recurring dream. I was strolling in the middle of a tree-lined street. I'd extend my arms and I'd take off like a bird. I felt elated, freed from the fears of an agitated childhood. I kept revisiting the dream. I later strapped on a parachute before taking to the sky -- a wise precaution as I began to develop engine trouble. The dream has since....

TITUS

You're shittin' me, man. This is no time for slapstick.

JEREMIAH, ignoring Titus

... the dream has since morphed into another gravity-defying stunt, something like levitation.

TITUS

Really?

JEREMIAH

Really. I jump up, each time higher, feeling ecstatic and proud of a feat that people on the ground find as startling as it is far-fetched.

TITUS

Can you blame them?

JEREMIAH

I detest indifference. Anyway, I take off and find myself at the threshold of deep space where cries are never heard, tears are never seen, and the human drama is all but a distant and nebulous distraction. I survey my home planet with a mixture of nostalgia, compassion and disquiet, suspended as I am at a point beyond time. I know I can never make a safe descent from that astral dimension. I think my time has come.

TITUS

You break my heart. I suppose you still indulge in these, uh... winged fantasies?

JEREMIAH, posing like a bird in
flight

Yes. I lean into the wind; my arms swept back to reduce drag, my fingers arched in a camber of my own design. I become airborne, a lone, tired gray eagle hitching a ride on some auspicious updraft. My takeoff is labored, the ascent shallow and sloppy. Gravity is a cruel foe, but I'm soon aloft. I'm now both winged night stalker and a spectator at my own air show.

TITUS, contemptuously

Sounds like escapism to me. Or is it idle bluster? Cowardice? Self-alienation? Or are these mere practice runs before the fall?

JEREMIAH

Old eagles ask no questions. They unfurl their wings and take to the skies where they belong. The sky shimmers with light. Other intrepid aviators lead the way. I'm not flying solo anymore. A fellow gray eagle....

TITUS

A fellow gray eagle.... How poetic.

JEREMIAH

... a fellow gray eagle told me that runways grow shorter as aviators get older. He died in his sleep just as he cleared the outer marker one early morning on his way to another dream. He now flies mercy missions in a small corner of heaven where dreamers get stranded. I shall be his copilot one day.

TITUS, exasperated

What kind of schmaltz is this? Do I look like an idiot? You better play along, pal.

JEREMIAH

O.K. Name your game but let's not keep score. I'm interested in the dynamics of game playing, not in trophies.

TITUS, a cruel gleam animating his
eyes

Only losers feel that way.

JEREMIAH

Victory and defeat are indivisible.
There can be no winner without a los-
er -- assuming there's something to
be won in the first place.

TITUS

Winning is the incentive of champions.

JEREMIAH

Dreamers have no passion for con-
tests.

TITUS, peevishly

Dreaming is an earned privilege, not
a right. You've exceeded your quota
and repeatedly violated the ban on
illicit dreams -- Article 404, Section 505, Paragraph 606 of the Uniform Dream Code. Why do you persist?
What the hell do you hope to gain?
What got you in this pickle anyway?

JEREMIAH

One day I awoke from a blinding tor-
por and discarded the last vestiges
of forbearance for senseless beliefs.

I rejected the notion that I was born sullied by some "primal offense," that pain ennobles the soul; that sentient beings need to be ruled by arbitrary, faith-based values and protocols. I'm referring of course to this ... this farce, your Dream Supreme World Order.

TITUS, now all ears

Yes, go on.

JEREMIAH

The Dream Supreme is an instrument of deceit and bondage. The bread it raises above the heads of born-again dreamers is a meal of false hope. The wine it bids us to drink is our own blood diluted by torrents of tears.

TITUS

You don't say....

JEREMIAH

I do say. Anyway, my conversion from fence straddling to mutiny was gradual, filled with misgivings. I was curious at first, but I found the mystique inscrutable. I meandered through its allegories and absurd doctrines like an explorer in a strange, uncharted land. I observed the very faint light this travesty claims to shed but I found only vast and gloomy shadows. It's in the shadows that my senses, now accustomed to the dark, caught sight of a glow that rinsed my pupils free of the gritty debris of credulity. I now knew that blind faith, *not* truth, prejudice and fear, *not* skepticism, threaten men and enslave them.

TITUS

Isn't skepticism a trap, isn't it?

JEREMIAH

Not nearly as confining as gullibility. Anyway, as my peripheral vision improved I realized that apathy, ignorance and stupidity invite everything from despotism to chaos. I witnessed these evils at close range wherever the dream commissars preside, where the steady erosion of civil liberties douses common aspirations and extinguishes popular will.

TITUS

And what did you do with this epiphany? Spread it around like poison?

JEREMIAH

Not at first. I took notes. I chronicled the miseries of the dreamless. Oh, how they suffered. For a time, the Dream Supreme's Sybil song was an enticing siren call but it didn't appease anger or restore sanity. It turned out to be a pre-washed, pre-shrunk, sanitized, one-size-fits-all dream scripted by the all-powerful and foisted on suckers and fools.

TITUS

And then?

JEREMIAH

Then, one day, I was invited by a local fraternal organization and asked to share my insights. The secretary who brokered the invitation urged me to steer clear of "forbidden dreams" -- no doubt a euphemism for vexing social issues.

TITUS

And did you?

JEREMIAH

Ah, *groupthink*! Isn't it amazing how the quest for harmony inhibits creativity and stifles independent thinking....

Fade out.

Interior. Office of secretary of fraternal organization.

SECRETARY, tactful

You see, we leave anything that might conflict with our members' personal convictions or sensibilities at the door.

JEREMIAH

But I don't do lectures on fly-fishing in the Ozarks or ostrich farming or trailer park humor or what the flag means to me. What I have to say is raw, graphic ... and ever so instructive....

SECRETARY

Do your best. Just keep it broad, keep it light. No sense agitating these good citizens.

Fade out.

Interior. Titus' office.

JEREMIAH

I grudgingly pledged to soften the rhetoric. Instead, throwing all caution to the wind, beguiled by the dream I was weaving, I let the audience have it with both barrels. I might have used greater restraint had my oration, delivered at the greasy spoon where local clubs meet once a month, not been preceded by tedious and silly pageantry.

TITUS

And that would be...?

JEREMIAH

I was first treated to a rousing chorus of Bless the Dream Supreme World Order, followed by a spirited rendition of the Dream Spangled Standard. I winced. Someone recited an ode praising the Grand Omnipotent Dreamer. I recoiled. Then came an invocation peppered with a chorus of Amen and Hallelujahs. The ceremony ended with the Oath of Loyalty, a ritual that always makes me cringe. The chaplain, his eyes shut tight, his head resting on his chest, his hands clasped over his crotch, offered grace. We sat down to an all-you-can eat lunch -- the obligatory slab of underdone fatty roast beef, a scoop of mashed potatoes submerged in rancid butter, five raw, fibrous string beans, a shriveled biscuit and a plastic goblet of synthetic lemonade. An Amazon of hefty proportions wearing a T-shirt proclaiming, *"I Only Take Orders from the Grand Omnipotent Dreamer,"* moved from table to table collecting "happy dollars." Everybody had seconds. I hardly ate. I remembered the vultures and the awful dreams they regurgitated.

Fade out.

Exterior. Sunrise. Tegucigalpa, Honduras. Vultures fidget on trees, preening their feathers. Some are poised on the tin roofs of shanties along the Choluteca riverbank. Others glide in wide sweeping circles like black-winged demons at a Witches' Sabbath, surveying life, anticipating death, smelling it, ready to swoop down on some irresistible morsel in the fetid dry riverbed below. Drawn by an irresistible stench, a scouting party makes landfall. Waddling from side to side as if inebriated, wary and cunning, they fight over scraps of offal. The leathery flutter of their wings sends chills down **Jeremiah**'s back.

> **JEREMIAH** (voice-over)
>
> I know what they're after. It's in this hellish chasm that the corpses of street children and other pariahs are dumped in the dead of night by paid vigilantes. Vultures eat well, far better than the wretched beings on which they feast ever did.

Fade out.

Interior. Restaurant meeting room. A dozen people are seated at a long rectangular table. Think of the Last Supper. The secretary opens the meeting and introduces **Jeremiah**, who is escorted by the sergeant-at-arms to the lectern. **Jeremiah** sizes up his audience -- a God-fearing American Gothic crowd, minus the overalls and the pitchforks.

> **JEREMIAH**
>
> Good afternoon. I'm known as Jeremiah and I get around. I attended a reception the other night at a posh hotel. I crossed paths with bejeweled women, most of them painted to camouflage the ravages of time. I shook hands with sweet-smelling, self-important

men in elegant double-breasted suits, silk ties and snake-skin shoes. I engaged in small talk and endured the syrupy banter between those who need to be seen and those who insist on being heard. Wealth, influence, power, all vied for attention as fragrant wines and succulent finger foods traveled on silver trays carried by white-gloved lackeys. Such flamboyance, I remarked, must be evidence of great virtue, the well-earned entitlements of the righteous, the uncorrupted.

Twelve pairs of eyebrows arch quizzically, mouths contorted by astonishment or a hint of suspicion.

JEREMIAH

Early the next morning, on my way downtown, where the uncorrupted never venture, I came upon sleepy-eyed children pulling heavy loads, sweaty *campesinos* packed like sardines in rickety trucks, half submerged under the provisions they bring to market from their distant hamlets.

JEREMIAH (voice-over)

In the stifling shadows of an aban-
doned hallway, young boys in tattered
clothes sniffed glue -- one way to
escape bad dreams. Further on, resting on a bed of filthy rags near the
gutter, a woman slept with an infant
at her breast while an older child,
disheveled, wiping an ever-runny nose
on her sleeve, begged for scraps of
food. And when I chanced upon the
sprawling municipal garbage dump I
found toddlers feeding on waste. I
asked myself what monstrous sins its
denizens had committed to deserve
such inexplicable fate. Gliding on
the wings of a sudden gust, a crum-
pled, lipstick-smeared paper napkin
landed at my feet. I recognized the
gilt monogram of the hotel where the
reception had been held the night before. I heard myself screaming.

Fade out.

Interior. Restaurant. **Jeremiah** leans toward a
corpulent woman busy chomping and wiping her
plate clean with a biscuit.

JEREMIAH

And how was the roast beef, Madam?

Visibly nonplused, people struggle to stay calm. Fidgeting in their seats, they look at each other, shaking their heads in disbelief.

JEREMIAH

Then, I met a living ghost. Homeless-ness robs people of all identity. Madness, in her case, further sharp-ens the alienation, the anonymity. She has no name and she will pass in this dimension and from this life un-noticed. Merciful, insanity yanked her from the clutches of her recur-ring nightmare. But she's real, the symbol and victim of the society that spawned her. Shunned, loathed, she inspires revulsion, not pity, for she is unrepentant, defiant in her gro-tesque cardboard palace, amid the de-bris, the scraps of metal, the offal on which she feeds, the useless memo-ries that haunt her still, come rain or come shine, come hell or high wa-ter. Ageless....

A man seated at the far end of the table stands up and raises his hand. **Jeremiah** looks at him absently and proceeds.

JEREMIAH

... ageless, toothless, feral and mad, she leans against a wall or steals forty winks on the naked pavement. Wielding a yard of rubber tubing or an old broom, she chases after man and specter, a menacing fist raised against oncoming traffic and snickering children, striking the ground with rage and bewilderment, spitting at passers-by, pelting them with invectives. Sometimes folly crests like an open flame and a torrent of tears drenches her grandmotherly face. Overwhelmed, she calms down, tunes in briefly on the world around her, a lifeless gaze now focused on an all-consuming void.

Then one morning, the police came and destroyed the paper, string and plastic shelter she'd erected. She put up a fierce battle but the cops prevailed. Trampled by uncaring feet, the decimated remains of her flimsy abode were carted away.

Up the road, in the narrow, wind-swept slop-splattered alley that hugs the flanks of St. Michael's Cathedral, a man writhed in drug-induced agony. Foaming at the mouth, his eyes on fire, he crumbled to the ground and let out a blood-curdling shriek. Thrashing about, wallowing in waste, he clawed at the demons that torment-ed him. Rolling onto the street, he narrowly missed being hit by a pass-ing car. Safe in their pews, their eyes turned heavenward, the faithful basked in the grand spectacle of a mid-day mass. *Dominus vobiscum*, chanted the priest. *Et cum spiritu tuo*, they responded, unmindful of the godlessness that surrounded them.

Around the corner, a group of cripples flaunted their grotesque in-firmities on the very steps of City Hall. Unruffled, passers-by stepped over them like so much rubbish. Across the street, a young woman breast-fed her newborn as three older daughters, sired by three different

men, plied the beggar's trade. Who
are the mad, I reflected, and who are
the meek who inherit the wind?

The women twitch and twitter and the men grouse
under their breath. The secretary, poor man, is
livid. Emboldened by an adrenaline-induced eu-
phoria, **Jeremiah** fires one last salvo.

JEREMIAH

Don't look for justice, ladies and
gentlemen. Don't look for civility. I
did. All I found are the aggregate
interests of the dominant power base.
Thank you very much.

The man who'd stood up earlier applauds polite-
ly but stops as he realizes that no one else
shares his enthusiasm. Ready to make a hasty
exit, averting **Jeremiah**'s gaze, people scramble
out of their seats. **Jeremiah** stops them and
points an angry forefinger.

JEREMIAH

One of you will brand me a heretic.
Eccentric old men who parade their
fondness for truth are more often
punished for their vehemence than for
their views. One of you will denounce
me and the Grand Omnipotent Dreamer
will try to extort a false confession
or squeeze out pledges of penitence.

One of you will insist that I'm crazy and demand that I be "therapeutically reformed." If I refuse to recant, I will be deactivated. Think of a clock that ticks but whose hands no longer move.

Jeremiah studies the surly faces around him. The "good citizens" file out without so much as a nod in his direction. The man who applauded whispers to **Jeremiah**

                    MAN

We must fear silence for it will keep the truth entombed.

Fade out.

Exterior. An eerie stillness fills the air. Vultures ride the thermals against a searing sky. The Dream Police knock at the door of **Jeremiah**'s apartment and hand him a summons.

          JEREMIAH, perusing the writ (voice-
                    over)

I earned the right to dream. But my score, **Titus** decreed, puts me in a "high-risk" group. He will only grant me a Temporary Dreamer's Permit. This entitles me to Class III dreams, safe, non-toxic middle-class fanta-sies that harmonize with sanctioned myths. I feel powerless, defeated, secluded. Loneliness is a merciless foe. It kills slowly, hope by hope, breath by mournful breath.

Fade out.

Interior. Titus's office. Titus stamps a document and hands it to **Jeremiah.**

                     TITUS
You should've let go of these dreams. Instead, you engaged in belligerent banter. You'll hear from us. Good day.

              JEREMIAH, (voice-over)
I thank **Titus,** mentally telling him to go fuck himself. I then blink him away. The dream shifts from anger to spite. It's so striking an apparition, so intense in its evocation that I mistake it for a nightmare I once lived. I revisit it, like a pilgrim at a sacred shrine, just to keep the memory alive.

Fade out.

Exterior. Footage from **2001 -- A Space Odyssey** (man-apes attack each other).

JEREMIAH (voice-over)

At dawn, they used their teeth, their claws. Later, they picked up a rock, a bough, a bone. They felt a power surging through their fists, and the carnage began. At high noon bombs began to rain. Fragmentation bombs rip, slash. Incendiary bombs scorch. Concussion bombs produce shock waves that shatter granite. Napalm, like molten lead, sticks to flesh and devours it.

(Flashback with footage of Kim Phuk, the little Vietnamese girl burned by napalm, as she runs toward the cameraman crying in horror and pain).

JEREMIAH (voice-over)

Some bombs spread the plague. Others paralyze, suffocate, blind. Neutron bombs snuff out dreams but spare monuments and shrines. Future munitions will target the poor, the sick, the mad; they will be programmed to obliterate certain races. Skunk works might even be developing a precision device that wipes out all graying men who engage in *belligerent banter*, ordnance that targets those who can't help but feel that more bombs are on the way, who say so out loud, and who warn that there will soon be no good place on earth left to hide.

Fade out.

Interior. Dream Licensing Bureau. Peering out of his 50-foot holographic overhead screen, the **Grand Omnipotent Dreamer** follows **Jeremiah** with his eyes as he exits **Titus**'s office.

GRAND OMINIPOTENT DREAMER

So, Jeremiah, tell me, what sort of utopian world do you have in store for us?

JEREMIAH, weariness slowly turning to anger

Every answer can be found in the question it evokes. Here's what I see: a world in which some have more than anyone could ever need to dream with dignity, while others prepare for the end of all dreams; a world where the old call upon the young to risk mutilation and disfigurement and madness, and where they die in their stead; a world where wars are waged to break the monotony of peace, where soldiers are feted for their murder-ous deeds with medals and ribbons and noisy parades, whereas common killers swing from the gallows; an imaginary society which presupposes that deity, private enterprise and personal initiative without oversight provides the greatest opportunity for achievement and progress.

The **Grand Omnipotent Dreamer** smiles but says nothing.

> **JEREMIAH** (voice-over) as the blood-red blaze of a nuclear blast spreads across the screen

Soon, the heavens will part. An eerie, all-consuming glow will turn the sky blood-red. A great stillness will hang over the devastation. Not a voice, not a murmur will be heard; not a thistle, a single blade of grass will grow. Emptiness will reign, vast, final.

Fade out.

Interior. In his apartment, **Jeremiah** peruses a newspaper as headlines and footage from police files unroll on screen.

> **JEREMIAH** (voice-over)

All the News That's Fit to Print. An

essay in Sunday's edition of the Dream Times sheds no light upon the heart of darkness. At best, it casts a distant ray on the realm in which evil breeds. This tedious chronicle of psychosis and brutality conveys astonishment, not horror, at a recurring reality: a cannibalistic serial killer, a mother baby killer, a mad bomber, a rapist, a pair of parricidal brothers, an adolescent child slayer. The litany only adds to the banality of evil. Evil is not unmasked. It's just put on exhibit in the pantheon of public voyeurism. Evil is ubiquitous, indelible. It's not "back," as the reporter claims. It never went away. If evil was an exploitable form of energy, the world would never run out of fuel.

Fade out.

SYNTHETIC VOICE

Jeremiah, Dream Identification Number 3579,you are hereby summoned at 10 a.m. on Friday, July 10 to appear before Case Officer **Titus**, to review irregular dream activity on the 12th, 13th, 17th, and 21st of last month, in violation of Article 404, Section 505, Paragraph 606 of the Uniform Dream Code. Pending appearance on said date, your Class III Temporary Dreamer's Permit is suspended. Reinstatement of privileges will hinge on the outcome of future interviews with the aforementioned case officer and at his discretion. Failure to appear on the due date will result in the irrevocable forfeiture of dream privileges, a fine, or a year community service as a grave digger. Repeated infractions will be dealt with in a manner consistent with the Uniform Dream Code. Penalties may include therapeutic reforming.

Fade out.

Interior. Jeremiah sits across **Titus**'s cluttered desk.

> **TITUS**, affecting affability
> I tried to warn you, pal. I'm not an unreasonable man. But you've got to cooperate. For your own good, if you

know what I'm saying.

JEREMIAH, with unmasked sarcasm

For my own good...?

TITUS

Let's see, where were we? Ah, yes. What happened when you first began to dream?

JEREMIAH

I spoke to my dreams. I tried to humor them.

TITUS

What did you say?

JEREMIAH

'*Let me help you,*' I told them with fatherly restraint. 'You can't be. You're brain waves gone AWOL. I can set you free. You'll never have to cross my mind again.'

TITUS

And what did the dreams say in return?

JEREMIAH

Dreams don't talk back. They just unfold at the frontiers of reason, persistent scenes of madness flashing before me, dissimilar yet linked by some elusive common thread. Like life.

Titus eyes an errant fly scurrying across his desk.

TITUS, bored
For instance?

JEREMIAH
Well, there's that damned old dream, early in the morning, seconds away from the alarm clock's merciless intrusion.

Jeremiah pauses, looking elsewhere.

TITUS
Go on.

JEREMIAH, hesitating
Some dreams are filled with so many abstractions, I'm not sure I can find the words.

Titus turns a glass over and traps the hapless fly. Then, smelling subversion, he snaps.

TITUS
What do you mean by *abstractions*?

JEREMIAH
I don't know; things that are felt but not easily put into words.

Titus stares at **Jeremiah** with beady bureaucratic eyes that conceal stupidity behind an air of smugness. He thumbs through the Uniform Dream Code but finds no entry for "abstractions." Leaning close to the glass, he peers through it as if it were a microscope. Close-up of **Titus**'s eyeball from fly's perspective. **Jeremiah** shuts his eyes for a moment, seeking the provenance of a sudden apparition. When he reopens them, **Titus** is shouting at him.

TITUS

Speak up, man. I'm listening.

Titus ogles the bewildered fly as it vainly struggles to breach its translucent prison.

JEREMIAH

I see thick gray smoke rising toward the wintry sky. '*I must live,*' a woman tells herself, not knowing why she thinks such thoughts. '*One more day, just one,*' she pleads. She will not close her eyes. The strength to reopen them might fail her.

Fade out.

Exterior. Auschwitz.

WOMAN (voice-over). Concentration camp footage.

'*It was summer, you remember? The rain made us laugh. We sang songs of joy and love and hope. The sign on* the gate has been freshly repainted. **"ARBEIT MACHT FREI,"** it proclaims with Teutonic concision.

                    JEREMIAH (voice-over)

She looks at the others, at their sunken eyes glassy with despair. Ghosts do not frighten her anymore. Why should they? She's one of them. The mud at her feet hides untold treasures. Prying stone from earth, lichen from frozen mire, she claws at the unyielding muck, breaking nails, drawing blood from withered fingers. Soon, she comes upon it. She spies her surroundings. She puts the muddy shard to her lips like a hungry infant to its mother's teat. Her mouth becomes wet with saliva and the drool oozes onto her tattered coat. She has her bone, still fresh, it seems, a splinter she can easily conceal. Who was it? Her son? Her daughter? Her husband? Perhaps no one in particular. Marrow has no personality. Protein is protein.

Fade out.

Interior. Titus's office

> **JEREMIAH** (voice-over)

Titus won't ask me to elaborate. He's too dense to appreciate metaphors. Paper pushers are innately obtuse. They have no imagination. They're phobic, unfocused, easily sidetracked -- or they'd become neurosurgeons or entomologists.

> **TITUS**, yawning

Do you have other recurring dreams?

> **JEREMIAH**

Many.

Titus races the glass back and forth across his desk with the fly still inside it, nodding occasionally as **Jeremiah** rambles on. He no longer takes notes.

> **TITUS**, absently

Go on, go on. Tell me more.

Titus awakens as if from a trance. No longer amused by the fly's desperate struggle, he rips its legs and wings, drops it on the floor, watches it writhe for a second or two then crushes it with the sole of his boot.

> **TITUS**, picking his teeth with a paper clip.

Stupid creatures shouldn't have the right to exist. By the way, do you dream in color?

> **JEREMIAH** (voice-over)

The asshole.

> Then to **TITUS**

How could I? I live a black and white
existence.

Fade out.

Interior. Jeremiah's New York apartment. Close-
ups of framed reproductions of Bosch's, Breughel's, Grunewald's and Durer's eeriest paintings lining the walls. **Jeremiah** entertains a
few guests.

> **JEREMIAH** (voice-over)

I tell them I collect paintings done
in insane asylums. Rare are those
sufficiently schooled to recognize
the geniuses who created them.

> **THE UNSCHOOLED**, scratching their
> heads

Hmm, very interesting *(says one)*.
Dear God, they're horrible *(says another)*.

> **JEREMIAH** (voice-over)

Nothing elicits banalities like dis-
comfiture or ignorance.

> **THE UNSCHOOLED**

Aren't you, um, droll. Painted in insane asylums.... That's a good one *(says one)*.

Or in the devil's workshop *(says another)*.

Exasperated, **Jeremiah** makes a circular gesture that enfolds the whole planet.

JEREMIAH

And what the fuck do you think this is?

JEREMIAH (voice-over)

If nightmares seem real at times, so does living, making dreaming a less offensive ordeal. Everyone is insane. Only the brave dare let go.

Fade out.

Interior. TV station.

TV COMMENTATOR

The superpowers have agreed to wage war for the next one thousand years or until their empires crumble -- whichever comes first. At regular intervals, nations will trade angry words. "Police actions," "preemptive strikes" and all-out wars of liberation will be fought, as usual, in other peoples' backyards, with or without their consent.

In the chill of open discord there's always time to prepare for the inevitable. The pact, fiendish in its minimalism, is founded on the premise that war is a morally justifiable deterrent against overpopulation. Thus, creatures that insist on multiplying, in the opinion of economists and social scientists, threaten the survival of the human race and must periodically be liquidated. Natural disasters, they assert, are rare, unpredictable and lack the cunning and inventive scale of man's death-dealing arsenal.

In preparation for the next round, Chinese dissidents are rounded up again and tortured while the swastika is resurrected and hailed in a "new" Germany disfigured by reunification. In the Balkan's tender underbelly, a neologism, "ethnic cleansing," deceptively sterilized, horribly banal, fails to attenuate the barbarism it evokes. Tribal war and AIDS in Africa's heartland add new resonance to the word *holocaust*. Power-starved Latin American colonels and corrupt puppet civilian regimes installed by the Dream Supreme Intelligence Agency feed popular discontent and foment dissidence so they can brutally crush it. Sikhs, Hindus and Muslims -- all convinced of the purity of their own creed -- set fire to a subcontinent devoured by illiteracy, poverty, class divisions, malnutrition and disease. And in the "Holy" Land, against all holiness and wisdom and compassion, fear, distrust and hatred make a mockery of the god the Jews invented, the Christians paganized and the Muslims conscripted and armed to the teeth.

Fade out.

Interior. Titus's office. **Titus** barely stifles a belch. **Jeremiah** fans the air with both hands.

TITUS

We're done for now. You'll be hearing from us.

Titus slams **Jeremiah**'s file shut and calls out,

Next!

Fade out.
Interior. TV studio.

TV ANCHOR

This just in: The New York Chapter of the Dream Licensing Bureau reports the seizure of an undisclosed number of contraband dreams destined for mass distribution in and around the metropolitan area. Characterized as 'morbid and subversive,' the dreams were impounded late last night in a raid on a dream-processing laboratory following a six-month undercover investigation by members of New York's elite Supreme Dream Enforcement Agency.

Dubbed Operation Pandemonium, the sting also netted training manuals. Parallel investigations by the Department of Dream Security also netted information on the tactics and makeup of a fledgling but elusive Dream Resistance movement.

Commenting on the seizure, one of the largest in recent history, a spokesperson for the Dream Liberties Union said that the steady rise in underground dreams reflects the mounting frustration of secular humanists with -- and I quote -- *'a sinister faith-based authority that grants a small clique of carpetbaggers dictatorial powers and turns governance into a marketplace of corruption and injustice.'* The National Dream Security Agency rejected the charge. Speaking on behalf of the agency, the **Grand Omnipotent Dreamer** had this to say:

Fade out.

Interior. GOD's office.

> **GRAND OMNIPOTENT DREAMER,** slowly, petulantly
> Purveyors of heresy are self-deluded blasphemers. Their psychotic rants must be silenced. We cannot allow them to infect an uncorrupted citizenry. The mutinous ideas spewed by the clarions of chronic malcontent

are designed to disfigure, desecrate and destabilize the ruling moral majority. They must be stopped. They *will* be stopped

Fade out.

Interior. TV studio.

TV ANCHOR

The **Grand Omnipotent Dreamer** declined to identify the producers and vendors of the impounded dreams, saying only that 'arrests and convictions are imminent.' If convicted, violators could face memory-erasing therapy or encoding, a procedure condemned by the dream rights lobby but widely practiced and with increasing frequency in schools and houses of worship.

In other news, an independent study reveals that a high content of dioxin, lead and mercury, as well as elevated levels of spent fissionable materials were detected in samples taken from seven playgrounds and four low-income residential projects built on landfill owned by the Dream Supreme World Order. Deputy Assistant Dream Director Spencer Shortstalk has categorically denied the study's findings. He blames a *'fifth column of miscreants'* but has declined to elaborate.

Fade out.

> **JEREMIAH** (voice-over)
>
> *"Never believe anything until it's been officially denied."* **Titus**'s cruelty haunts me still. I replay the spectacle over and over. Evil has no cause, only effect. It was just a harmless fly, free, inquisitive, capable of power dives and barrel rolls and dead-stick loops and chandelles and gravity-defying inverted spins no human pilot could ever execute....

Flashback. Interior. Titus's office.

> **TITUS**
>
> *'You gotta land sometime, don't you?'*
>
> **JEREMIAH**
>
> *'Yes, to refuel.'*
>
> **JEREMIAH** (voice-over)
>
> ... a lowly insect stunned by the ag-

ony of confinement, crazed by dismemberment, now wingless, flightless, struggling to fathom the horror, writhing uselessly, reflex animating a desperate kinesis, the last cadence of life that a paper-pusher named **Titus** -- judge, jury and executioner -- mercifully ends with the sole of his boot.

It is so vile an image to contain that **Jeremiah**'s skull distends and bursts like an over-inflated balloon, scattering fragments of dreams, projectiles of unreason and the twisted debris of insufferable grief to the four winds.

Fade out.

Interior. Jeremiah's apartment. Early on the morning of July 10, four uniformed agents led by Inspector Langford T. Hunnicutt, of the Dream Enforcement Agency, rouse **Jeremiah** from an exceptionally pleasing dream and haul him before the Second Circuit Dream Court.

Interior. Courthouse.

MAGISTRATE

Jeremiah, also known as **3579**, you are charged with crimes against the Dream Sedition Act. The four-count indictment cites insubordination, counter-culturalism and iconoclasm with intent to poison the hearts and minds of the compliant majority. How do you plead?

                    JEREMIAH

Not guilty.

                    MAGISTRATE, peeved

You don't really mean that.

                    JEREMIAH

I do.

                    MAGISTRATE

You don't seem to understand....

                JEREMIAH, addressing spectators

Oh, I understand. His honor doesn't tolerate innocence. In his court a presumption of innocence is a costly liability, not so much for the accused as for the system. He prefers guilty pleas. They're less thorny, easier to adjudicate. In his court, where free thought is the moral equivalent of treason, where dreams are on trial, a guilty plea helps speed things up. One can't be acquitted in his court without damaging the reputation and authority of the Dream Supreme.

MAGISTRATE

"A man who represents himself in court has a fool for a client..." We'll provide counsel if you so desire. If not, you're on your own. Have you been so advised?

JEREMIAH

Inspector Hunnicutt took noticeable pleasure in pointing that out.

MAGISTRATE

Are you sure you wouldn't rather wake up and ponder the soundness of your plea? Think of the burdens of innocence, the liabilities. You can recant, you know. If I were in your shoes, I'd reconsider.

JEREMIAH

You've got to be dreaming....

Magistrate looks at **Jeremiah** with contempt. All **Jeremiah** sees reflected in his icy glare is the emptiness of zeal.

MAGISTRATE

Very well. Go ahead.

JEREMIAH

The Dream Supreme World Order ... can't stand disorder. It must rule without hindrance. To prevail, it must govern by decree, heaping laws and rigid injunctions on exhausted and demoralized citizens in an ever-tightening spiral of repression. Like all despotic systems, it aims to brainwash the masses. Children are its first and most promising sub-jects. Schools now require that tots memorize slogans and aphorisms often found in fairy tales. The clichés they implant in young impressionable minds have little to do with morality or patriotism. They're not meant to inspire but to instill skewed values and launder away every last molecule of precocious curiosity, imagination and free will a child might possess.

MAGISTRATE

You're stalling. Get to the point.

JEREMIAH

I'm referring to that popular and charming parable, *The Cicada and the Ant*. Its underlying message has the power to subvert the young and turn them into legions of compliant adults.

MAGISTRATE

Stop filibustering or I'll have you declared in contempt.

Spectators hum with anticipation. They all carry a copy of the famed allegory. It's the Bible of the moment, the *Little Red Book,* the Upanishads, the sacred Buddhist teachings, the all-purpose chaplet of prayer beads.

JEREMIAH, restive

Ben Franklin said, *"The way to see by faith is to shut the eye of reason."*

MAGISTRATE, to court reporter

Strike that. (Turning to **Jeremiah**) We're convened to review and adjudicate your case, not to quote a Freemason and irreligious libertine.

JEREMIAH

Karl Popper warned that Utopia tends toward despotism. Mario Vargas added....

MAGISTRATE, chortling

Popper...? Poppycock. Ours is the ideal society, the model state.

JEREMIAH

...Mario Vargas added that the idea of a model state is the trademark of monsters. They're more likely to be places of privilege for the well-to-do and cash cows for greedy speculators.

MAGISTRATE

I'm warning you.

JEREMIAH

Your honor, we're here to pay homage to a humble insect -- misunderstood, misrepresented and maligned. My defense is anchored in a simple expression of sympathy and esteem. I refer to the cicada, the modest, seventeen-year locust that chirps all summer long then dies of hunger come fall. I plead on behalf of that lumbering, un-aerodynamic aviator that frolics from tree to tree and croons in search of a mate. And I give you the common backyard ant whose sole mission is to hoard provisions in a race against time and looming winter. Diligent, focused and resilient, the ant has only one objective: orderly survival. It knows nothing else. It toils from dawn to dusk, from birth to death, never once veering from its appointed task. The cicada just keeps on singing, unmindful of its mortality, unaware of the lean days and perils of winter. The first autumn chill finds the cicada destitute and famished. You know the rest: it knocks at the ant's door and begs for a scrap of food.

'And what did you do all summer while I was hard at work gathering provisions?' asks the ant.

'Why, I sang,' replies the cicada.

'You sang, well, hey, dance now!' And the ant slams the door on the bewildered cicada.

The gallery roars with delight.

MAN IN SPECTATOR GALLERY

That'll teach that bleeding heart cicada lover.

JEREMIAH

Yes, your Honor, the cicada's summer is brief, a one-movement symphony, an ode to joy, the triumph of indifference over the immutability of death.

The ant lives on to serve the colony. Only death frees it from its mindless bondage. Could it be that life rushes by as time stands still for insects too? Could it be?

The magistrate has as much perspicacity as a filet of mackerel. Suspicion narrows his eyes into two cruel slits.

MAGISTRATE

What kind of question is that?

JEREMIAH

Oh, nothing; just thinking out loud.

Spectators snicker and mimic **Jeremiah.**

WOMAN

Yeah, just thinking out loud. Why don't you keep your thoughts to yourself and go on with your lamebrain defense, Jeremiah.

JEREMIAH, annoyed but self-possessed
You're all suffering from reflex myopia. You've been programmed to believe that ceaseless and exhausting work gives the ant security and freedom from persecution, whereas the carefree cicada deserves its misfortune because it is stupid, lazy or

unimaginative. Controlled, brain-washed, granted limited rights but given enough slack to create an illusion of freedom, ants, like men, labor their life away to fatten the queen and serve the colony. They survive in a perpetual state of aimless agitation. Soldier ants will die on some remote battlefield. Worker ants will age before their time. Neither the queen nor the colony will ever acknowledge their sacrifice.

MAN IN GALLERY

Traitor! Pinko agitator! Communist!

JEREMIAH, unflustered

It's the fate of ants to work like robots. It's the lot of cicadas to fill the air with their serenade. Neither is really in each other's way. Instead, that awful parable glorifies the drudgery of ants and instills disdain for the free-spirited cicada. It also....

SPECTATORS

Booo! Turncoat! Conniver!

JEREMIAH

... It also telegraphs the monstrous message that self-perpetuation and mindless toil merit praise, whereas the brief rhapsodic summer of cicadas is without worth or honor. No! Slave labor does not ennoble. Art is not trivial. By promoting intolerance, egotism and miserliness, your syllabus romanticizes evil.

Fade out.

Exhausted, out of breath, **Jeremiah** wakes up in his bed in a cold sweat. The dream, vivid and all-consuming, arouses new fears of retribution. Being on the defensive prevents him from savoring the pleasure of not giving a damn.

Fade out.

Interior. Top-floor office, somewhere in Manhattan.

MAN in office

I'm not familiar with your work but your reputation precedes you. Dreaming is a lucrative endeavor and the harvest is as rich as it is varied. It's impossible to keep up. No sooner has one crop of mind-blowing ideas fed the ravenous dreaming elite than new seedlings take root. Dreamers are such a fickle lot. They never seem to dream enough. It's an addiction. Anyway, let's talk about you. You discovered a new window through which dreams may be observed and....

JEREMIAH

I've done nothing of the kind. I'm a contrarian, not a revisionist. I promote dreams that make windows superfluous. I'm not sure I succeeded. You know, dreams don't always have the final say. The insights they impart must be jettisoned to make room for new ones. Every scaffold, every joist and beam and casement they tear down, every layer of paint they scrape off, every obstacle they surmount ... leaves a void that must be filled so it can be emptied again and again. Learning must involve a certain amount of *unlearning*.

MAN

Are you saying that windows get in the way of reason?

JEREMIAH

In a manner of speaking. Regardless

of its orientation, a window offers only a narrow view. If it takes more than one window to apprehend the totality of things, why bother?

MAN

Are doors as restrictive as windows?

JEREMIAH

You can live without a window if you must; a door is a necessity.

MAN

Assuming windows and doors shield against the elements while affording only an incomplete view, would you ban the use of windows?

JEREMIAH

Would I deny a blind man the use of a flashlight?

MAN

I see what you mean. You say you're working on dreams that make windows unnecessary. Please explain -- unnecessary to whom?

JEREMIAH

To those willing to see the world without them, those capable of discarding conditioned beliefs, those who seek to dream their own dreams.

MAN

There are risks....

JEREMIAH

Sure, and dreamers must assume them. But half of something is better than all of nothing. Better to fail than be denied the right to try; better to dream than sleep. Better to stumble and fall than schlep to someone else's drumbeat. But don't worry. Dreamers are an endangered species. They'll continue to stir the world's collective conscience but they won't prevail. Not yet.

MAN

What do you mean?

JEREMIAH

I once asked Ayn Rand if she'd been preaching the virtues of selfishness because it exists in such abundance, because compassion hinders natural selection. Ayn Rand shrugged and begged to be excused from the dream. I later challenged Pascal: Is it possible, I ventured, that *'the govern-*

ment of one's being,' as he so grimly described life, rests in a single dream? But Pascal sneered at the thought, branded me a heretic and damned nearly had me burned at the stake, had I not managed to wake up just in time.

MAN, awkwardly

I can see where your dreams might seem heretical. Free thought has its downside. But rest assured: I don't always favor mainstream views, if you know what I mean. I'm a pragmatist. Anyway, looks like you've broken new ground. Your findings could help us reach our long-term objectives.

JEREMIAH

Objectives?

MAN

Surely, dreaming without 'windows' is an achievement that is light years ahead. But we seek to go further still.

JEREMIAH

Further still?

MAN

Yes, we aim to do away with dreaming altogether. Don't be shocked. Hear me out. We're working to eliminate the *necessity* to dream. We're looking to foster a state of serenity that makes dreaming superfluous, that overrides reality.

JEREMIAH

Forgive me but your concept is flawed and regressive. Think about it. The perfect dream does not shield us from reality; it brings us closer to the threshold of a *better* reality. It's anticipation in its purest form; it's hope distilled.

MAN

How so?

JEREMIAH

You said, '*We're striving for a state of mind that makes reality more desirable than dreams.*' Have I got that right?

MAN

Yes.

JEREMIAH

What do you mean by *state of mind*? What is serenity? What is reality? Whose reality? You're not out to eliminate dreaming at all. You're out to clamp on a new set of windows, to reframe reality, to circumscribe the limits of consciousness and alter human experience on the basis of a single narrow view. The road to hell is still paved with good intentions, isn't it?

MAN

But....

JEREMIAH

Sure. There were others. Moses dreamed up a set of rules that we defy with every breath we take. Jesus hallucinated with schizoid self-predestination. Caesar's *Pax Romana* was extorted at the point of a sword and the Republic fell. The prophet Muhammad branded the souls of his converts with a ham-fisted -- pardon the un-kosher pun -- brutal imitation of the Judeo-Christian pipe dream.

Disunity and war eclipsed Napoleon's vision of a unified Europe. Karl Marx called for equal distribution of goods produced collectively. Poor Marx, he forgot that greed gets in the way of kindness, that ideals are devoured by ideology. So Stalin and Mao took over Marx's dream and turned it into a nightmare that nearly erased mankind's last hope for redemption. Hell-bent on creating a master race and robotizing a nation, Hitler shattered millions of dreams and befouled Germany's image for the next one hundred generations. They all invaded our dreams, aiming to impose their standards of reality on a world that breeds with reckless abandon and can barely feed itself. Men never do evil so fully as when they do it from conviction.

MAN

But surely, in a way, weren't these men dreamers too?

JEREMIAH

No. They dished out nightmares. Real

saviors let the world decode their dreams. These men were led by ego, ambition, narcissism, arrogance, a lust for power, control, influence. They weren't dreaming. They weren't content to entertain their own vile thoughts. They decreed that everybody must tune in on their frequencies or die; follow in their footsteps or be crushed; embrace their values or fall from grace.

MAN

You mention Jesus. Wasn't he, as Nietzsche suggested, a political criminal?

JEREMIAH

Nietzsche spun his own dreams. Who am I to argue with him? The body politic is the real 'criminal.' No. Jesus was a misguided dream merchant whose fixations became corrupted by the collective folly and spiraling fanaticism of his disciples. He wanted to share a vision of goodness and tolerance and compassion. Instead, more blood was shed in his name than flows

in humanity's veins. Good Christians
should **imitate** Jesus, not worship
him. The coward's way out is to adore
that which he cannot emulate. Pretense and self-delusion are such cozy
asylums. And yours, sir, is just another scheme to commit us there.

MAN

Please understand, uh, this is not *my*
scheme.

JEREMIAH

No, it's the scheme of the Dream Supreme World Order. But you condone
it, you endorse it, you promote it,
you let it trample you. You write off
the institution but you embrace the
ideology that created it and the
mindset that sustains it.

MAN, ill at ease

Well, uh, I work here, you know. I
need this job. It helps pay for other
dreams. There's the kids' college tu-
ition, the new redwood patio, the
swimming pool, last summer's dream in
the Seychelles. I still owe a chunk
on the BMW and the basement needs wa-

terproofing. Monique, my youngest is
being fitted for braces. Martha, my
wife, says she's due for a facelift.
Look at her....

Man points to (and camera zooms in on) the fam-
ily portrait on his desk: Martha, resplendent
in her hair-sprayed bouffant hairdo; blemish-
free, freshly-scrubbed all-American features:
lily-white skin, generous curves; a figure that
bore three freckle-faced children, all girls,
and would have borne more had the necessity to
pay for other diversions not diluted her husband's libido. Her husband: crew cut, mono-
grammed, button-down white shirt and vested
steel-gray pin-stripe suit; a gold Rolex and
ringed pinkie. Their offspring: three homely
blue-eyed tubby young girls with bovine expressions, carbon-copies of the Aryan ideal. **Jeremiah** regurgitates the man's feeble exculpation.

> **JEREMIAH**, (voice-over)
>
> *"... This is not my scheme."*
>
> **JEREMIAH**, quoting Thomas Paine
>
> *"When a man has so corrupted and
> prostituted the chastity of his mind
> as to subscribe his professional be-
> lief to things he does not believe,
> he has prepared himself for the com-
> mission of every other crime."*

Fade out.

Interior. Courtroom.

BAILLIF

The Second Circuit Dream Court is now in session. All rise.

MAGISTRATE

Be seated. Bailiff, call the first case.

BAILLIF

The defendant will face the Court.

MAGISTRATE

Jeremiah, Dream Identification Number 3579, you are accused under the Dream Sedition Act of crimes against the One Dream World Order. Charges include third-degree insubordination, second-degree counter-culturalism and first-degree interstate dream commerce with malicious intent to subvert mankind. How do you plead?

JEREMIAH

I repeat, not guilty. Free thought and humanism and secularism are on trial here, not I.

MAGISTRATE

Strike that last remark. Free thought is a hallucination. Humanism and secularism are mutinous concepts designed to confuse and corrupt the loyal elements of a duty-bound socie-ty. Now, **Jeremiah**, are you prepared to resume your defense?

JEREMIAH

I am.

MAGISTRATE

Begin.

JEREMIAH

Begin you. Justify the charges.

MAGISTRATE

Nay, you must begin. Refute them.

Wild-eyed, knitting furiously, corpulent house-wives and their blathering progeny -- the sows and the screech owls -- occupy front row seats.

JEREMIAH

As water can't feel wetness or fire sense the burning flame, so a dream can't perceive itself. It just is.

Jeremiah pauses, scans the gallery and returns the insolent stares and uncomprehending smirks of the spectators.

MAGISTRATE

Proceed.

JEREMIAH

You're all wondering how it began. In the early morning hours of September

16, I was jolted back to sobriety by the sound of shattering glass. When I reached the jagged hole in the window of my hotel room, Emile Rousseau, with whom I'd been drinking all evening, lay dead on the pavement below. His eyes were wide open. A faint smile etched his bloodied face. I remember wanting to weep. I didn't, I couldn't.

MAGISTRATE, mocking

You'll have plenty of time to weep. We'll make sure of that.

A mean collective chuckle rises from the spectator gallery.

JEREMIAH

I stood by the window, unable, unwilling to move, compassion and self-pity tugging at my psyche, mixed echoes of pain and folly and death booming inside my head.

Fade out.

Exterior. A small medieval town in France shrouded in a fine, lace-like mist. Clouds hang low, coalescing with steam rising from the rain-slick flagstones dotting a hotel's courtyard. Church bells toll in the distance.

Fade out.

Interior. Courtroom.

JEREMIAH

I bowed my head then I looked up, well above the highest spires, past a certain point in space where God is said to dwell. Cut against the pallid halo of a receding moon, there it stood, spectral and uninvolved -- the King's Lair -- where Rousseau's dreams and mine first converged.

MAGISTRATE

Is this a travelogue or a defense summation?

JEREMIAH

Just a few pertinent facts, your honor. By day, even from afar, the King's Lair looms like a mythical vessel, a stone *Flying Dutchman*, ghostlike and inaccessible, suspended in a distant haze.

Fade out.

Exterior.

JEREMIAH, (voice-over as camera surveys the scenery he depicts)

Larger than life, the castle appeared, stilled by time, frozen in space. Austere, if not sinister, it dominates a rambling patchwork quilt of red tile and slate rooftops, sculpted gables and pepper pot turrets. Huddled against the stony ramparts like barnacles on a sunken hull, houses hug narrow, winding cobbled streets, squares and arcades. Here and there, forged iron catwalks and humpback timber bridges straddle an ageless river.

Fade out.

Interior. Courthouse.

JEREMIAH

It's across these ancient spans and along meandering alleyways and cul-de-sacs that mystics and lepers, vagabond monks and alchemists, merchants and knights and poets of yore once lived, journeyed, battled and died. And it's in the shadow of that gray citadel, where "holy" inquisitors tortured sinners and broke their spirit to save their soul, that I went mad, so to speak -- or as the indictment purports. No, I didn't throw myself, wild-eyed and foaming at the mouth, on innocent bystanders with a cleaver. I didn't set myself on fire on some crowded public square. I didn't swat at imaginary flies, or babble incoherently, or claim to be King Solomon or Julius Caesar. No, my brand of lunacy, I'm told, is infinitely more heinous: I apprehended a new way of looking at the core of things. I opened a mental eye heretofore blinded by conformity and, as dreams go, I killed for his trouble -- and at his request -- Emile Rousseau, the man who showed me the way.

MAGISTRATE to spectators

You'll all agree that once acquired, such knowledge can never be unlearned, thus making Jeremiah's crimes all the more egregious.

Spectators rise to their feet, raise their fists, stomp their feet and rumble their displeasure.

SPECTATORS

E-gre-gious, e-gre-gious, e-gre-gious....

MAGISTRATE

Order in the court!

JEREMIAH

You're right. The truth can't be un-learned. That's why it's relentlessly concealed or suppressed by those who fear contamination. For the truth is an infection, isn't it, a soul-devouring abscess, stealthy, resili-ent, all-consuming, often lethal.

Spectators hiss. The magistrate raises a concil-iatory hand.

MAGISTRATE

The *infected* can be... *disinfect-ed*.... We have the means. We won't allow them to sow our fields with fresh seeds of folly. We won't let them play hide-and-seek. We won't let their ... castles in the sky obstruct our horizons.

Spectators chortle. Sarcasm is sweet ambrosia to the rabble.

JEREMIAH

Disinfected? You mean re-programmed, dismantled, undone, rendered useless, don't you?

MAGISTRATE

Call it what you will. Proceed.

JEREMIAH

There was a time when a home was truly a man's castle -- and castles are my dreaming hobby. You can ask Kafka. I write about them, about their lodgers and I often spend weekends in some drafty, high-ceilinged bedchamber just to hear the dreams their tapestry-covered walls have to tell. Such was the purpose of my mission when, on September 9, I set out to explore the King's Lair.

It's from these heights that vats of boiling oil and cauldrons of molten lead -- suitably sanctified with a sign of the cross -- were poured on raiders below, all of them wielding assault weapons that had been similarly consecrated.

Between sieges and battles and

beheadings and bouts of pestilence, feudal lords hunted in the thick forests that once covered much of the land. At night, under the quivering light of torches and candles, the great hall came alive with feasting and dancing and performances by jugglers, minstrels and soothsayers, some of whom were fed to the dogs for fumbling, singing out of tune or foretelling less than a perfect future. *Noblesse oblige*.

MAGISTRATE

Skip the history lesson, Jeremiah and get on with your plea.

JEREMIAH

When Rousseau and I met late that afternoon, our dreams merged and our futures came undone. I'll never know who paid the higher price. Nor can I forget the way he invaded my dreamspace, uninvited, annoying like a neurotic Chihuahua or a recurrent itch. His eyes were red, his eyelids puffy and damp. His nose was running. A yellowed cigarette butt dangled from a blistered lower lip. He reeked of wine.

'Spare a few coins, *Monsieur*? It'll set you free,' he ventured cagily, as if ready to back off, to retreat from the irreverence of a vacant stare, the humiliation of a snub, defenseless against indifference, accustomed, if not immune, to avarice and scorn.

I stopped, dug into my pockets, averting his eyes. He didn't fit the part but he had that look that beggars have which is best unacknowledged, a liquid gaze in which float the cadavers of hope, will and purpose, a lifeless glare oozing with despair. I handed him all my change. It wasn't much. I mumbled an apology and walked away. He followed, ambling along sideways like a crab, tugging at my sleeve.

Fade out.

Exterior. Town park.

ROUSSEAU

Hey, don't fret, *Monsieur*. Me, I accept anything. I'm not picky. It all adds up. A fraction of something is worth more than all of nothing, if you know what I mean.

Uniformed groundskeeper winks at **Jeremiah**, a telling forefinger drawing circles around his temple.

GROUNDSKEEPER

Pay him no heed. **Rousseau**'s harmless. He just talks too much; must have been a lawyer or a salesman in some previous dream. Anyway, panhandling is forbidden. Don't encourage him.

Jeremiah ignores the groundskeeper and turns to Rousseau.

JEREMIAH

I'd have been that much poorer had I given any less. Charity for the sake of easing one's conscience is no charity.

ROUSSEAU

Oh, but that was no charity I took, *Monsieur*. I made an investment. You wait and see.

GROUNDSKEEPER

All right, Rousseau, that's enough.

Move on. Clear out. Make way.

ROUSSEAU

Some people never see the light, even if it blinds them.

Groundskeeper mutters an expletive, turns on his heels and walks away.

ROUSSEAU

Trust me, giving is a profitable en-deavor. The giver never loses.

Fade out.

Interior. Courthouse.

JEREMIAH

I looked at **Rousseau,** intrigued and troubled; mostly troubled.

Fade out.

Exterior. Town park.

JEREMIAH

Who are you?

ROUSSEAU

Me? An apprentice. A time voyager. Like you. A fellow dream-chaser.

JEREMIAH

How long have you been on the road?

ROUSSEAU

Forever, it seems.

JEREMIAH

When will you stop?

ROUSSEAU

When I get there.

JEREMIAH

There? Where is *there*?

ROUSSEAU

Who knows? There's a fork in the road. One path is unmapped and rarely journeyed. Call it a dispensation.

JEREMIAH

A dispensation ... from what?

ROUSSEAU

From the burdens of reason.

JEREMIAH

And the other?

ROUSSEAU

The other is well traveled and the shortest path of all.

JEREMIAH

The one that invades other people's dreams, I suppose.

ROUSSEAU, with sham sorrow

How unkind. No, no. Shorter still.

JEREMIAH

Well?

ROUSSEAU

The climax of all dreams. Death, what
else.

Fade out.
Interior. Courthouse.

JEREMIAH

It was my turn to peer into Rousseau's eyes, to decipher the message
they telegraphed. A sudden rain
drenched the battlements before us.
We stood there, dripping wet, locked
in a brief and inscrutable stare,
connected it seemed by some indefina-
ble kinship that dusk and the elements cut short. I blinked, even as I
dreamed, and rubbed my eyes. Rousseau
had vanished like an apparition, a
specter, leaving behind a trail of
unease and foreboding.

Exterior. At a distance, in full view of a
group of tourists, perhaps in their honor, the
groundskeeper unzips his pants, pees on the
moss-covered stone parapet, readjusts his beret
and navy blue cape, mounts an old bicycle and
rides away.

Fade out.

Interior. Courthouse.

MAGISTRATE

I think it fitting at this time to
call for a fifteen-minute comfort recess.

Fade out.

JEREMIAH, (voice-over)

And so the Magistrate raps his gavel
and retreats to his chambers. The
Bailiff escorts me to the men's room
where I discover that the "*loyal elements of a duty-bound society*" fart
when they piss, that they bend their
knees to take a crap like the rest of
us, that they seldom wash their pat-
riotic hands, that they're capable of
gutter humor and nasty gossip, that
they blithely parrot, as if it were
their own, the hand-me-down opinions
of generations of Babbitts who wrap
themselves in the flag in a futile
attempt to rise above their own medi-
ocrity.

Interior. Courthouse.

JEREMIAH

The next time we met -- more by intu-
ition than chance -- at the very spot
in the dream from which he'd faded
away, Rousseau offered to 'set me
free,' if I agreed to reciprocate.

Fade out.

Exterior. Town park.

ROUSSEAU

You're my last hope.

JEREMIAH

What are you talking about?

ROUSSEAU

Hear me out.

JEREMIAH, pushing Rousseau gently aside.

I'm not interested. Now, if you'll
excuse me.

Jeremiah walks away but Rousseau thwarts his
escape and grabs him by the arm.

ROUSSEAU

Salvation has its price. Free me from
these bonds and all I know is yours.

JEREMIAH

Your kind of knowledge is of no use
to me. It kills.

ROUSSEAU

So does ignorance.

JEREMIAH

Not with as much refinement or malice. I've listened to you patiently. Now you listen to me. I don't know how or why, but you've managed to raid my dreams. Lucky Rousseau. Crafty incubus. The likes of you hunt for fresh quarries, impregnate them with their bitter seed and devour them from the inside, isn't that right?

Rousseau shakes his head and falls silent.

Fade out.

Interior. Courtroom.

JEREMIAH

Rousseau had reached an impasse but it was I who felt lost, vulnerable. Strangely, his rhetoric had seduced me, luring me through its occluded symbolism like a diver surrendering to the rapture of the deep. I felt drawn not by the faint light this strange little man shed along the way but by the shadows from which he'd emerged. I found his ideas beguiling and terrifying. I was overcome with a mixture of curiosity and fear. A part of me wanted to obliterate Rousseau, to end the dream; another longed to make sense of the man, to decode his cryptic insinuations.

I returned to the dream armed with questions begging to be answered, doubts put to rest. Was Rousseau mad? The groundskeeper thought so. So did I, although I suspected that lunacy had in some way sharpened his intellect. I knew there are ill-defined forms of psychosis, so subtle, so skillfully concealed, and so utterly undetectable that they elude even those trained to recognize the thousand faces behind which they hide. Is he insane who pretends to be lucid? Is he who fakes madness -- crazy? Is rational behavior evidence of sanity? Are boxers bashing each other's brains out of their minds? Are the fans salivating at the prospect of blood, of a bone-crushing knockout deranged too? Is faith in an invisible, unknowable "God" a form of psychosis? Are citizens who vote into office inept or corrupt politicians in full possession of their faculties? Or are they imbeciles who deserve the thugs and clowns they elected? Is the soldier who fires at an enemy he can't see behaving rationally or, to dilute the horror -- or ease his conscience -- is he pretending to be shooting blanks every time he squeezes the trigger? If not, if he finds moral justification in sanctioned murder, or derives some secret thrill from it, is he demented, evil or just a hopeless moron? Everything....

SPECTATOR

Anarchist! Radical!

JEEREMIAH

... Everything about Rousseau was a necrology, an obituary written in advance of a suicide by proxy. Rousseau lived to eliminate Rousseau. Life to him was a post-mortem. But he was also a terrorist who took pleasure in spreading melancholy and unease. His words inspired visions of reality that surpass reality itself.

MAGISTRATE

And you keep straining the limits of this court's patience. I'm warning you, Jeremiah.

JEREMIAH

Your Honor, this preamble is crucial. Anyway, I kept to my hotel room for three days and three sleepless nights. The King's Lair, the legends, the mysteries, everything I'd planned to explore, to immortalize, would have to wait. Rousseau was on my mind. I should have been able to dismiss him as a demented bum who preys on those who show compassion, a pervert bent on polluting the gullible, the lost, the vulnerable. But I couldn't do that without questioning my own sanity. I was seized with a horrible thought: Was he *me* in some remote corner of time? Was I *him* in a parallel dream?

MAGISTRATE

Well, was he, were you?

JEREMIAH

Who knows? I hated Rousseau but I thrilled at the images and sensations his mantra inspired. I'd been helped up the tree of knowledge and left dangling from its highest boughs. Only the fear of falling kept me from savoring the view. Suspended as I was between chaos and order, aware of their kinship, confusion turned to terror: Was I mismanaging this dream?

At nine on the night of the 16th, I heard a knock at the door.

'Entrez,' I said, expecting the chambermaid with an armful of fresh towels and the evening paper. The door creaked slowly open. It was Rousseau, sober, clean-shaven, sporting a suit of questionable vintage, a pink rosebud pinned to his lapel. He held two bottles of wine in each hand. A chessboard was tucked under one arm.

Spectators fidget and whisper among themselves.

Fade out.

Interior. Hotel room.

> ROUSSEAU

May I?

> JEREMIAH

What do you want?

Beaming, **Rousseau** holds up the wine bottles as if they were trophies.

> ROUSSEAU

Let's celebrate the dream, let's you
and me turn the grapes of bitterness
and sorrow into the wine of amity
over a friendly game of chess.

> JEREMIAH

I don't drink much and I'm lousy at
chess. How did you find me?

> ROUSSEAU

Mon ami, I didn't have to go far.
This is a very small dream.

> JEREMIAH

How did you make it up to my room?

> ROUSSEAU

I took the stairs.

JEREMIAH

God damn it, that's not what I meant,
and you know it. How did you get
passed the concierge?

ROUSSEAU

Madame Tiler? Oh, she's having supper. I dashed past her lodgings. Be-
sides, it's late in the season.
You're the only registered guest, you
know.

JEREMIAH

I didn't know. And I don't care.

ROUSSEAU

Well, here we are. You wouldn't let
an old lush like me polish four li-
ters of *Pomérol* all by himself, now
would you?

Fade out.

Interior. Courtroom.

JEREMIAH

Rousseau looked more wretched in his
weather-worn, oversized tweed suit
than he had when he first entered the
dream, disheveled, unshaven, in tat-
ters and drunk. He'd gone to great

lengths to look respectable. He would have looked out of place in white tie and tails at the wheel of a Bugatti. Poor man.

Fade out.

Interior. Rousseau's hotel room

> **JEREMIAH**, reluctantly

O.K., come in.

> **ROUSSEAU**

Thank you.

Rousseau walks into the room, uncorks a bottle and pours the crimson brew. He takes a long and avid swig and wipes the corners of his mouth on his sleeve. He then places the chessboard on the coffee table and removes the pieces from his coat pockets -- black from one, white from the other.

> **ROUSSEAU**, rubbing his hands

You're head of state, general, feudal chieftain, shah. This is war. Two armies are poised to fight to the finish. Your kingdom is at stake, to be sure, but so are your wits for they lead the battle. Defeat me and victory is yours.

> **JEREMIAH**

What if I lose? I've never won at

chess or any other contest, not even in a dream.

ROUSSEAU

There's always a first time. But if you lose, you still win. Victory is often hollow but defeat is never in vain. Failure has the makings of a potential success.

JEREMIAH

And what if I win?

ROUSSEAU

Well, make sure that victory doesn't contain the seeds of defeat.

Fade out.

Interior. Courtroom.

JEREMIAH

It took Rousseau less than an hour to beat me. We played three more games; I lost them all. It must have been the wine. Rousseau had polished nearly two bottles though he seemed none the worse for it. I was inebriated. Inebriation makes me silly. Drunkenness renders me stupid. Emboldened by defeat, I said, 'One more game.'

Fade out.

Interior. Hotel room.

> ROUSSEAU

Haven't you had enough?

> **JEREMIAH**

Not enough to make me feel like a winner. Isn't that what you promised?

> ROUSSEAU

A real winner only loses once. To lose once is noble. To lose twice is rash but forgivable. To lose three times or more as you did is reckless.

> **JEREMIAH**

I'll win this time. This time I *want* to win.

> **ROUSSEAU**, taunting

Wanting is not enough. If you lose *this time*, you lose for good.

Jeremiah takes another swig.

> ROUSSEAU

You can't beat me. You know why? You won't let yourself.

> **JEREMIAH**

Nonsense, I tell you. Just watch me.

                    ROUSSEAU

If you lose -- and you will -- you
must go the distance. You must forfeit something.

                    JEREMIAH

Like what?

                    ROUSSEAU

My life.

                    JEREMIAH

Come again?

                    ROUSSEAU

You must sacrifice me.

                    JEREMIAH

You're nuts. Your move. Play.

                    ROUSSEAU

A deal's a deal. Remember, you invest
in me. I empower you. We'll both reap
the dividends.

                    JEREMIAH

You're jesting.

              ROUSSEAU, sardonically

I'm dead serious.

Fade out.
Interior. Courtroom.

                    JEREMIAH

Rousseau laughed maniacally. But his

eyes were glazed, lifeless, impenetrable.

Fade out.

Interior. Hotel room.

ROUSSEAU

I'm at my journey's end. Any more
dreaming will simply spill over, uselessly, wastefully. Set me free.

JEREMIAH

If you're so keen on dying, why don't
you take an overdose or blow your
brains out?

ROUSSEAU

You don't understand. I long for one
final act of charity to compensate
for a lifetime of indifference
and....

JEREMIAH

'*Charity begins at home.*' Do yourself
in if you must but don't look at me.

ROUSSEAU

What, and forfeit the terror or the
rapture or the chilling apathy on my
killer's face? Pass up the scorching
ferocity or the icy composure or the

disdain, or perhaps the hopeless look of guilt and shame in my savior's eyes?

JEREMIAH

Savior? Forget it, Rousseau. I'm not your man.

ROUSSEAU

But you are. Look inside yourself.

Fade out

Interior. Courtroom.

MAGISTRATE

Good heavens, man, what are you saying?

Bewildered, spectators fidget and look at each other.

Fade out.

Interior. Hotel room

ROUSSEAU, capturing a bishop

I must die a violent death. I must taste the horror. Let death be life's last passionate embrace. I want to see it coming, feel its grip as it submerges, then drowns out reason and switches off the senses. Do you hear me?

Jeremiah nods absent-mindedly, sacrificing a rook, a knight and his queen in rapid succession.

ROUSSEAU

Do you hear me?

JEREMIAH

Stop it. You can't make me.

ROUSSEAU

You have no choice. This is your dream.

Fade out.

Interior. Courtroom.

JEREMIAH, agitated

'*I have no choice, this is my dream*,' I hear myself mumbling. Like a bad gambler I covet defeat. I'm drunk. Deep down inside I lust to please Rousseau and, in so doing, to obliterate him once and for all, to trash his memory like a redundant computer file, to keep him out of my dreams.

So I lose another game. Anger floods my veins, searing my body with an unholy fever, a fury born of confusion and shame, a rage that hides

other emotions, like spite and humiliation and fear. Rousseau looks at
me. A cruel gleam animates his eyes.
No, it's not cruelty; it's something
else, a mixture of eagerness and
scorn.

Fade out.

Interior. Hotel room.

JEREMIAH

I won't do it. This nightmare must
end.

ROUSSEAU

You have no choice.

JEREMIAH

You're insane. Get out of my dream,
damn you, you're crazy.

Jeremiah beats his fists against **Rousseau**'s
chest. **Rousseau** kisses **Jeremiah** on the mouth.
Jeremiah grabs **Rousseau** by the throat and
squeezes. Jeremiah's eyes fill with tears.

ROUSSEAU

'*Everyone is insane. Only the brave
dare let go.*' Isn't that what you
said to your guests in an earlier
dream? Isn't it?

JEREMIAH, startled

How did you know?

ROUSSEAU

We're all toiling in the devil's workshop, aren't we?

Flashback of earlier scene during which guests gape at Jeremiah's paintings.

Fade out.

Interior. Courtroom.

JEREMIAH

Rousseau looks into my eyes and his eyes are bright like those of a child beholding a rainbow. I squeeze a little harder. His eyes close for a moment then they reopen and in them I see my reflection.

Fade out.

Interior. Hotel room.

ROUSSEAU, gagging, looking skyward, praying

You are my shepherd. You carry the lamb on your shoulders. Night is falling. Come hither. He who wounds me deepest loves me best.

Weeping, **Jeremiah** pushes Rousseau clear across

the room.

JEREMIAH

God help me.

ROUSSEAU

Help yourself, Judas, my brother.
There is no God. Help yourself.

Rousseau crashes through the window and falls to his death.

Fade out.

Interior. Courtroom.

BAILLIF

All rise.

Sound of bodies straining to shuffle out of their seats.

MAGISTRATE

Be seated.

Sound of bodies straining to squeeze back into their seats.

MAGISTRATE

You're an ugly man, Jeremiah.

JEREMIAH

Why, because I tell the truth?

MAGISTRATE

No, because you take sinister pleasure in dredging it, dishing it out,

flinging it in our faces as if it were swill.

JEREMIAH

You confuse duty and pleasure. The truth often stinks. Should I have de-odorized it first?

MAGISTRATE

It would have made it less jarring to those who sample it for the first time.

JEREMIAH

So you're conceding that I might be telling the truth?

MAGISTRATE

I concede nothing. I was referring to *your* version of truth.

JEREMIAH

The truth is a bitter pill. It must be swallowed whole. It must chafe your gullet as it goes down. It must burn your entrails. It must sear your soul with shame and repentance before it can ever begin to repair the ravages of credulity.

MAGISTRATE

And so you've taken it upon yourself

to shed the dark, cold light of your own apostasy?

JEREMIAH

The truth reveals itself to those who look for it. It helps turn the ignorant and the duped against the merchants of delusion. Your doctrines are divisive, exclusionary and despotic. They belong in the home and the prayer houses where discounted dreams can be had for the price of obedience. They have no business anywhere else.

MAGISTRATE

Rebel dreamers fan public unrest. They want to be perceived as advocates of justice.

JEREMIAH

And demagogues pretend to protect the ignorant and the naïve in exchange for their obedience.

A low, rumbling hum rises from the spectator gallery. The women are all atwitter. The men are flummoxed.

MAGISTRATE

How dare you! *'Ignorant'* you call them? No. Strong in their convictions? For sure. Naive? Nonsense. Passionate? Devoted? Steadfast? Yes! Yes! Yes! Have they not the right to fly the flag and put their faith in the Almighty? Are they not....

JEREMIAH

The Almighty and the flag form a wretched team. They've broken every record for tyranny and violence.

MAGISTRATE

... are they not the loyal servants of our noble Dream Supreme, the righteous who obey the Word that brings redemption and unity and moral vigor and reverence and love for the one true cause? Are these not the brave warriors who battle perversion and wickedness and iniquity and evil? Why, they are the very salt of the earth, I tell you.

JEREMIAH

Any truth that owes its existence to blind faith is a lie.

MAGISTRATE

I say that only the teachings of the Dream Supreme lead to the truth.

JEREMIAH

And I say that your ritualized theatrics and mumbo jumbo turn fragile psyches into helpless robots.

MAGISTRATE

And I respond that you, Jeremiah, are a superfluous heretic, a distraction and a purveyor of sorrow.

JEREMIAH

Without heresy, the salt of the earth can find contentment only in their colossal ignorance.

Out of breath, flush with anger, the magistrate waves **Jeremiah**'s dream journal.

MAGISTRATE, slamming the journal on his desk.

It's all here! Venom! Filth! Blasphemy! Our Dream Supreme World Order is mankind's only path to salvation.

JEREMIAH

Your brand of salvation consigns people to lives of despair.

MAGISTRATE, pointing at the spectators.

The righteous dwell in palaces of chastity as they await final passage to that supreme dream not woven by human minds. Behold. Don't they look superb? Aren't they the embodiment of decency and goodness and solidarity and mutuality of purpose?

JEREMIAH (voice-over)

I'd always associated sermons with stirring orations on the perils of sloth and lust and gluttony and envy and ire, on the dignity of the poor, the larceny of kings, the debauchery of the clergy, the degeneracy of the aristocracy and the inescapable brevity of life. When did courtroom proceedings turn into pious harangues? Preaching tends spontaneously toward inquisition.

Jeremiah surveys the spectator gallery and catches sight of a phalanx of snarling *Madames de Farge* and *Inspecteurs Javert*, men in plaid trousers, striped shirts, checkered jackets and baseball caps. Poised like tigers eyeing prey, matronly women with bouffant hairdos glower at him. They all cheer the magistrate or weep ecstatically, breaking out in fervid salvos of Amen and Hallelujah as they throw their arms in the air and sway in trancelike unison.

JEREMIAH, pointing at various
spectators

I see creatures of habit who fear change, despise scholarship, cling to the status quo; depend on it. It is with horror that I recognize in their collective fervor, in their truculence, the same blind adulation, the same abject submission that millions of drooling Neanderthals showed the little Schicklgruber in beer halls and city streets and parade grounds. I remember the visage, the din and thrall of intolerance. Noble souls? I see a conclave of diehards. I see in their body language the robotic impulses of androids. I smell war on their breaths.

A loud, angry cacophony soars from the gallery. Human faces morph, Mr. Hyde-like, into snarling, foaming, fang-bearing lupine jaws.

MAGISTRATE

You're trying to destroy treasured ideals. Forget it. It won't work. Give up while you can.

JEREMIAH

You mean turn the other cheek? The

last time I did that I was beaten un-
conscious. No. I don't negotiate with
fanatics.

Red with anger, a spectator leans over the
railing and yells at **Jeremiah**

SPECTATOR

You've got some nerve! *You're* the fa-
natic.

JEREMIAH

No. I'm defending against the insidi-
ous theology you're promoting. I'm
guarding against a catechism honed to
corrupt minds, enslave souls and pick
pockets. I'm resisting the impostors
who profit from the naiveté and blind
faith of their quarries, parasitic
dream-snatchers that graft themselves
onto unsuspecting souls.

MAGISTRATE

Should I remind you that you once
shared our vision?

JEREMIAH

Shared? Shared? Never! I ignored it,
foolishly, that's all. Then I saw the
light.

MAGISTRATE

Have you no shame, no reverence for
the sanctity of the Dream Maker, no
regard for our beloved Dreamland?

JEREMIAH

You find me at a disadvantage. Piety
is an alien emotion and nationalism a
toxic psychosis I learned to fear as
a child. I dread both the concepts
and their motley incarnations.

The magistrate frowns. His face scrunches,
conveying a grim blend of indignation, bewilderment and incomprehension. He blinks a cou-
ple of times and falls silent.

JEREMIAH

Your honor, I am, therefore I dream.
I dream, therefore I doubt. The more
I doubt, the more secure I am. The
blind, the deaf, the mute all conspire against the truth for they
would have you seek it through their
eyes, their ears, their twisted, im-
potent tongues.

Spectators squirm in their seats.

JEREMIAH

As for the truth with a small *t,* ladies and gentlemen, it's your turn to

unearth it. I tried. This tribunal
has been convened not to silence the
screams but to stifle thought. The
truth is a solid line but no one
bothers to seek out the individual
dots of which it is comprised. For
here, under these artificial lights,
here is the end of the line.

MAGISTRATE, smirking

Now, now. Things could be worse, you
know. We could rouse you out of your
dream. But let's first take a fifteen
minute recess.

Spectators jump out of their seats and rush to
the toilets. The sound of stomping feet whisks
Jeremiah away to another region of the mind
where tangential dreams are spawned.

Fade out.

Interior. Insane asylum.

JEREMIAH (voice-over)

I wake up tasting blood, my tongue
savagely bitten in the course of a
dream that has run amok, an exquisite
hallucination that, this time, earns
me a stint at the Dream Rehabilitation Center.

Fade out

Interior. Asylum cafeteria. Lifeless, like the eyes of a dead fish, poached eggs stare back at **Jeremiah**. The **Grand Omnipotent Dreamer** materializes stereoscopically in the eggs. He beckons **Jeremiah** to draw near and, as he does, the **GOD**'s face looms larger in the viscous yolk. He smiles his synthetic smile and revels in its unctuous hypocrisy.

> The **GOD**, looking up from inside the eggs.

Well, well, if it isn't Jeremiah. I hear you've been flying, *here and there*.... But you had to make landfall, didn't you? Only this isn't a regularly scheduled refueling stop, is it? Looks like you've been grounded. No doubt some grimy dream clogging up the old engine. Or is your inertial navigation system, uh, inert? You could have stayed home -- a new SUV in the garage, a season's pass at Shea Stadium, a subscription to Reader's Digest, a bubble bath with your sweetheart in a champagne glass-shaped Jacuzzi at a nice hotel in the Catskills.... But no! Jeremiah can't sit still, can't shut up, won't repent. Common aspirations aren't good enough. He's got to chase after his own cockeyed dreams.

JEREMIAH

What's worse -- unraveling fact from fiction and exposing the lies, or shielding them from scrutiny?

The GOD

Hasn't internment tempered your foolish dreams? Hasn't it cured the wanderlust?

JEREMIAH

A change in scenery tempers very little, least of all wanderlust.

The GOD

In times of crisis, and against the likes of you, we have the right, the duty to....

JEREMIAH

The crisis is of your own making. You've turned this self-granted "right" into a license to suffocate dreamers.

Jeremiah pokes the yolk. A runny **Grand Omnipotent Dreamer** liquefies and spreads over the sausages and home fries.

Fade out.

Interior. Courtroom

MAGISTRATE

Jeremiah, This court finds you guilty on all counts. You're charged with crimes against the Loyalty Act, con- spiring to provide support to sedi- tious elements, reckless failure to heed the counsel and warnings of the authorities. You're further accused of taking part in acts of dream diso- bedience and in sowing the seeds of conflict while undergoing treatment at our rehabilitation center. Given the severity of your crime, the mag- nitude of your apostasy and the great risk of recidivism, you are hereby sentenced to be deactivated. Designed to silence subversion, this radical and irreversible procedure will be carried out at oh-six-hundred tomor- row. May the Grand Omnipotent Dreamer have mercy on your soul. Have you an- ything to say?

JEREMIAH

The cruelest form of tyranny is perpetrated under the shield of law and in the name of justice. *Silence subversion?* Don't you get it? When you hear nothing but the hush of censorship, you have a cover-up and the lingering scent of putrefaction.

MAGISTRATE

You're not helping your case.

JEREMIAH

Do what you will but I'll speak up until I leave this world the way I entered it -- one unaware of the other, mutual indifference etched upon the other's face. In the end, dreams are like matter. They're indestructible. Once dreamt, they live on in the collective memory of those they visit, inspire or agitate. They travel on long and tireless caravans that link those yearning to break free. Someone always rallies from afar to reinvigorate the dreams. They breed and mutate and proliferate.

Fade out.

Interior. TV studio.

ANCHOR

Intelligence programs will be the main beneficiaries of federal spending, according to a new study released by the Office of Dream Management and Budgeting. The study reveals that the counter-dream intelligence market is likely to exceed $10 trillion by the end of the decade. Two programs are expected to boost the Dream Supreme World Order's surveillance capability: seek-and-destroy dream reconnaissance satellites and mind manipulation technology.

Fade out.

Interior. Courtroom.

MAGISTRATE

Jeremiah, your time has come. Are you ready? Have you made peace with your maker?

JEREMIAH

I fear no abstraction, however absurd. I fear the tyranny of man. I fear conceit. I fear the creed that justifies the sacrifice of martyrs at the altar of piety.

MAGISTRATE

Feisty words from one fated to silence.

JEREMIAH

Words have a way of resonating long
after the dream-teller is gone.

MAGISTRATE

Who do you think you are?

JEREMIAH

I am what I think but I'm incomplete
if what I think is left unsaid.

MAGISTRATE

Trust me, *your* words will be forgot-
ten. They don't have the ring of
sanctioned truth.

JEREMIAH

To the deaf, nothing rings true except what they choose to hear. They
never get past the voice of their own
bigotry and hatred. If I erred, it is
for having misjudged events. This is
an occupational hazard. Fortunately,
unlike doctors, high priests and com-
manders-in-chief, our casualties do
not end up in body bags.

MAGISTRATE

Dreamers don't know everything.

JEREMIAH

You're right. And we're the first to admit it. But we search, we probe, we explore. We crave for knowledge. You, on the other hand, have stopped searching. You've wrapped yourselves in the security blanket of ignorance and shut the door tight against the very light of knowledge, and you won't let anyone pry it open.

MAGISTRATE, gesturing to a stage hand

Suit yourself. This is your closing scene. It's curtains for you.

JEREMIAH

You're wrong. The show *will* go on.

MAGISTRATE

Poor fella, you're delirious. We won't prolong your ordeal. It's customary before sentence is carried out to grant one final request. You have three choices: a full-course meal of your own confection; a one-night conjugal visit; or one last dream. What will it be? Speak now.

JEREMIAH

I'll take the dream.

MAGISTRATE, snickering

I knew you would. Expect it to leave
an aftertaste.

JEREMIAH

Can't taste worse than these proceedings.

Fade out.

Interior. Jeremiah's heavily damaged Manhattan
apartment. Walls are cracked, furniture broken
and upended. Drapes flutter against shattered
windows through which a scene of utter devastation unfolds. Close-up of **Jeremiah** at debris-
covered desk, pen in hand, his dream journal
spread open before him. His face is caked with
dust and scarred with welts and lesions His
eyes are red. Blood oozes from his ears and
nostrils.

JEREMIAH (voice-over)

A year ago, I fell asleep in the tub
and dreamed that I was taking a bath.
It'd been a rough week. Another war
had erupted, this time too close for
comfort. The prognosis was poor.

War is a profitable business but
it's often the result of miscalcula-
tion, not design. No one really wanted war, no one was quite ready to

wage it, let alone win it. In time, words got sharper, less guarded, and weapons, the antithesis of reason, grew deadlier with each sound bite.

No one protested very loudly. Not a single voice rose against the demagogues who beat the drums of war. No one dared send to hell the politicians who champion it, the economists who justify it, the bankers who finance it, the industries that thrive as it rages on, the generals who prosecute it -- while the rest of us imbeciles are forced-marched to the front to die or be maimed or driven mad in the name of some cockeyed grand dream. Even the professional dissenters kept quiet, their intellect sedated, their vocal cords muted by fear or waning conviction. It felt as if a malignant tedium, a pervasive apathy had replaced common sense.

Sporadic at first, famine spread like wildfire. Infant mortality skyrocketed. There were other casualties. What little food could be scraped to keep the heart pumping proved less than enough to nourish the mind. Two billion people suffered irreversible brain damage. Insane asylums were full. More were desperately needed to contain a swelling tide of mental illnesses but none was being built and the overflow spilled onto the streets, along with the homeless, the sick, the dead and the dying.

At home, men 17 to 59 were training for the front or patrolling the streets. Everyone was armed. In the cities, the haves wrangled with the have-nots. Looting, assaults and other acts of violence soared during the long hot summer and thousands died at the hands of vigilantes, mercenaries and roaming bands of thugs. Justice was blind to injustice. Anti-war activists clashed with flag-waving diehards happily too old for conscription.

Basic staples -- bread, milk, eggs -- were in short supply. Meat, when available at black market prices, was rarely fresh. But hunger subverts reason and everyone took chances. If hunger and exposure killed the poor, it was often food poisoning that claimed those who could still afford to eat. Not unlike ants, we spent the fall hoarding and digging in deeper. A calamitous winter lay ahead.

At Uranus Press International, where I now dreamed for a living, wire service reports kept a skeleton crew on its collective toes. I had double-shifted for over four months, shuttling between decoding room and rewrite desk. If we could no longer manipulate dreams, the editor had decreed, we would milk them to the last drop. Anything to sell dreams. Anything.

I was worn out. Only a bath, steaming, filled to the brim could relieve the tension and wash away the toxic thoughts that overwhelmed me.

Fade out.

Interior. Jeremiah stretches in his bathtub, water up to his chin.

> **JEREMIAH**, to camera, extreme close-up
>
> I remember closing my eyes, my mind slowly shifting into neutral as I surrendered to sleep. I can't tell you my astonishment, my unease when I reopened them and discovered -- straddling the commode, breeches down to his ankles -- Jerome Van Aken, the noted artist and social commentator. He was reading a comic book and I was conducting an interview for the midnight edition with a celebrity who was taking a dump in my bathroom. It was not an easy assignment.

Van Aken dressed in 15th century attire, sits on the toilet, leafing through a copy of *Mad Magazine*.

> ### JEREMIAH
>
> Many delight in your work -- I for one. Others, shocked by your unerring view of the world, call it morbid and indecent. Their words, not mine.

Van Aken unrolls several sheets of toilet paper and blows his nose.

VAN AKEN

My work and I have been called many
things. I pray the polemic lives on
after me. It nurtures my self-worth.
We use mirrors to feed vanity, never
to regard ourselves as we are; which
is why the images they send back are
always inverted.

Van Aken strains to relieve himself. **Jeremiah**
looks at his visitor through wisps of steam
rising from the tub, noting his complexion --
furrowed and coarse like that of an old mariner
-- studying his thin, stubborn mouth, the cleft
chin, the distant Delft-blue eyes now staring
in the void.

JEREMIAH

Turning abstractions into crisp,
terse copy, as my editor demands, is
beyond my faculties. Would you mind
translating?

Van Aken tosses the magazine across the tile
floor and lights a cigar.

VAN AKEN

Skip it.

JEREMIAH

The eroticism that drenches your
paintings, their eccentricity, the
bizarre juxtaposition of good and

evil, devotion and impiety, reason and folly -- all keep tongues wagging, ink flowing, psychologists parsing and dissecting every scene, critics critiquing. But none ever seems to get it right, do they?

VAN AKEN

Critics get paid to trivialize what they don't comprehend, what they're incapable of creating. It's their nature. They enjoy shaping public opinion by the light of their own prejudices. Anyway, the world *is* physical, sensual, erotic. Or else we wouldn't be here. As for my perceptions, only I can perceive them with any degree of clarity. The public and the critics have my work. The rest belongs to me.

JEREMIAH

Do you think sex is a trivial, perfunctory pursuit, as some of your canvases tend to suggest?

VAN AKEN

Not at all. But let's face it, if the ultimate reward of lust were not in the fleeting pleasure it delivers, do you think anyone would indulge in such grotesque gymnastics?

JEREMIAH (voice-over)

I searched for words. But the dream wouldn't have it and the words came out wrong. So I changed the subject and asked the question that had haunted me since I'd first laid eyes on Van Aken's riveting images. I'd discovered small details, hints that were both prophetic and eerily familiar.

JEREMIAH

When did the blindfold come off?

VAN AKEN, startled but receptive

After I alit from the middle chamber, died at the hands of three ruffians, was raised from the grave and agreed to travel, seek further light and impart it. Just like you.

JEREMIAH

In whom do you put your trust?

VAN AKEN, smiling

In myself.

JEREMIAH

Do you believe in a supreme being?

VAN AKEN

In the beginning there was man. And man created God in his own image so that man may trudge in ceaseless doubt, the better to contemplate the enormity of his own ignorance. I'm still in transit. The journey is long and fraught with danger. Thinking about God reinforces the concept but it doesn't lend it substance.

JEREMIAH

What do you mean?

VAN AKEN

Ask yourself: What *"intelligent designer"* remains stone-silent while the sobs of men are never heard? What *"ineffable"* entity is this, whose ear is deaf to the throngs who call on him and seek his succor? Who is this *"God"* who never shows his face, never bares his heart, never sheds a tear, never says he's sorry, a God who grants life and, with it, the fear of dying?

JEREMIAH

So where's the truth?

VAN AKEN

No formula can deliver all truth, all harmony, all simplicity. To see everything through a single window would leave us seeing nothing. If only we could tear down the walls that fence us in, break the shackles of intolerance. If only we could do away with the creeds that divide and debase us.... But why do you ask?

JEREMIAH (voice-over)

Van Aken hated interviews. He'd never granted one before. Were it not for the dream I was weaving that evening, I doubt he would have talked to me, much less taken a shit in my toilet. But Uranus Press International planned more layoffs, so I did what I was told, even if it was only in a dream.

JEREMIAH

Some of your characters are loathsome, yet they inspire pity, not hatred. What a bewildering contrast.

VAN AKEN

Can you name anything more bewildering than life, more unfathomable than
the human condition?

JEREMIAH

The brutality that colors their lives
is sharply offset by their pokerfaced
expressions. They look stunned but
they show no emotion. It's as if they
were wearing masks.

Van Aken yawns, spreads his legs wide apart
and peers into the toilet bowl.

VAN AKEN

They are dazed, stupefied, that's
all. When one suffers, it's just a
matter of degree. Pain travels but it
never really goes away.

JEREMIAH

Sodomy is a recurring feature in your
work, what with the people you skewer
with bird beaks and trumpets and har-
poons and giant corkscrews and....

VAN AKEN

Art imitates life. We've all been
buggered -- by our leaders, by *free
enterprise,* by money lenders and

civil servants, drill sergeants and car salesmen, the stock market, bosses, coworkers, even by our friends and fellow-travelers.

JEREMIAH

Is this the voice of experience or metaphor?

VAN AKEN

I don't use metaphors. I observe. Centuries pass and we keep on lecturing the simple-minded, punishing heretics, pinning medals on the chests of professional killers, executing vulgar amateurs, enacting unenforceable laws, preaching unworkable ethics. And when our lords and masters decide a little war is overdue, we let them drag us into battle. We pray for victory. We bless the juggernauts. We kill. We plunder. We die and others take our place -- the young, the hope of all our tomorrows. There's the depravity, the reeking immorality of it all. Should I paint pink angels and fat-assed cupids and drooling mystics staring heavenwards in stupor?

JEREMIAH

Is someone so disenchanted with life afraid to die?

VAN AKEN

Death is an inconvenience to those who savor the sensation of being. But that's life.

JEREMIAH

Does it take courage to *be*?

VAN AKEN

Yes. But once we *are*, the courage to be is undermined by the fear of *not being*. Perhaps if we could sneak a peek at the fullness of reality from the void of nonexistence -- from the womb so to speak -- we might wisely opt not to be. I know I would. But to an apprentice one lifetime is not enough. There's still so much to do. Reality must be given form: on canvas; in rhyme; set to music; carved out of granite and marble and bronze. We must then hope that the truths reality delivers brand the soul, cauterize it, that the warnings it issues are heeded once and for all.

JEREMIAH

You contradict yourself. First you disavow the human race then you rush to its rescue.

VAN AKEN

Posterity gets in the way. I wish to be remembered not for my style but for the truths my paintings endeavor to unveil.

JEREMIAH (voice-over)

Van Aken's cautionary tales are mitigated by pity for his fellow humans who can find no moral home within themselves. His art is all the more unique in that he does not portray man in his spiritual power or physical strength but in his inner weakness, fragility and vulgarity. Van Aken lays bare the contradictions of his age. His work is an outward meditation on the irreparable sadness of the soul, on the brittleness of the spirit, on the longings that haunt us, the unfulfilled dreams that leave us disheartened. Above all, he reminds us that life is a ceaseless struggle toward self-affirmation.

Van Aken shifts fretfully from side to side on the toilet seat.

JEREMIAH (voice-over)

Van Aken's words struck home in a strange, unsettling way, with verve and lyricism. But my editor didn't want verve or lyricism, just drama, no matter what it took to fabricate it. So I switched from the sublime to the ridiculous.

JEREMIAH

Have you ever considered running for public office?

VAN AKEN

Don't make me laugh. There are no lasting convictions in politics, only temporary accommodations shared by a privileged few who keep manipulating our destinies under the pretext that we grant them that right. I want no part of it. My work is my ballot.

JEREMIAH

What do you mean?

VAN AKEN

Democracy is not a sustainable system. Not in the long run. Remember, Athens crumbled. Its noblest attributes, the ideals it purports to espouse, the very freedoms it champions -- all enfeeble it: it tolerates in its bosom the existence and proliferation of undemocratic ideas. It sows the seeds of its own demise. The more freedom men achieve, the more they abuse it. Think of an organism whose parts, in order to survive, conspire against the whole; picture Medusa devouring itself. It's a mesmerizing spectacle. The symbiosis is fatal in the end.

JEREMIAH

So what's left?

VAN AKEN

What's left? Uncertainty. The thrill of impermanence. Randomness and bedlam. Rebels and despots trade places until it's impossible to tell them apart. The world will continue to produce would-be redeemers bent on saving us -- or else. The spider will spin her web, the sun will rise, the cockerel will proclaims the birth of a new day, and we will spurt out of our mothers' bellies, wet and cold, only to thrash about for a time on battlefields and assembly lines, while the tax collector....

JEREMIAH

Your views are tinged with rancor. Have you ever been tempted to end it all?

VAN AKEN

Have you ever read Camus?

JEREMIAH

Yes.

VAN AKEN

The Myth of Sisyphus?

JEREMIAH

Yes; and *The Stranger*.

VAN AKEN

Well, then you know that life is absurd and meaningless and that death comes all too soon. So why not live and enjoy the consternation we seem to cause, you with your dreams, I with my art?

JEREMIAH

Were it in your power, what would you change?

VAN AKEN

It's not in my nature to reflect on the past, except to revisit an attic full of dust-covered dreams. One thing is clear. Man is selfish; he suffers from selective amnesia and rarely learns from his mistakes. But let me ask you -- how do *you* think history will judge us?

JEREMIAH

History is written and redacted by men. Take out their biases, their inferences, and history is little more than a boring compendium of facts and dates. But things have changed since the advent of live news coverage. History now unfolds in real time. Social scientists view history as an evolution from savagery to sophistication. We dreamers are far less upbeat. Men struggle; they live in fear, turmoil and madness. Let's impeach the cretins, the killers and the kleptocrats we elect, but let's also denounce our own stupidity. *"Those who can make you believe absurdities can make you commit atrocities."*

VAN AKEN

Yes, victors blue-pencil history to justify and exalt conquest, losers to blunt defeat. Neither side will concede the other's account. The hostility such conflict invites often leads to other assaults, other defeats.

JEREMIAH

Are we all insane?

VAN AKEN

We are. But we'll keep on feigning sanity. It helps dress up our lives. If acting is the art of pretense, living is the science of deceit. We do a bit of both now and then and sometimes it's hard to tell which is which.

JEREMIAH

Are we doomed?

VAN AKEN

Yes, but not literally. Mankind can't tolerate itself so it will keep on multiplying. It's a form of self-punishment. Life feeds upon the innocent. The supply is inexhaustible.

JEREMIAH

One last question: How real is this dream?

VAN AKEN

Real enough. Imagine if men were judged not just for their deeds but for their secret thoughts, their dreams, their hankerings: dungeons and madhouses would be full.

Van Aken flushes the toilet and **Jeremiah** wakes up.

Fade out.

Interior. Jeremiah's extensively damaged apartment.

JEREMIAH (voice-over)

Granted, I'd dreamed before. I'd soared like an eagle, tumbled from a thousand cliffs. I'd been eaten alive, smothered by hideous witches astride my chest, castrated by jilted mistresses, torn limb from limb by monsters of my own creation. I'd even drowned in shit. Nightmares come in many hues and textures, and I'd worn them all. This last uncensored dream was something else. The Magistrate was right. It did leave an after-taste, like Strontium-90; or Cesium-137.

It's been a year now but the dream haunts me still. I know Van Aken would have empathized but he died 500 years ago when the Renaissance freed man from ignorance and superstition, lifted him halfway between matter and spirit and sent him roaming in search of himself. Better known as **Hieronymus Bosch**, what he saw was prelude and climax in an age of nascent enlightenment and persistent folly. What he foretold was the recurring death of reason: The Inquisition. Colonialism. Slavery. Famine. Pestilence. Wars of *"liberation."* Wars of conquest. Fratricide. *"Holy"* wars. *Wars to end all wars.* Genocide.

Weapons of mass destruction. Death squads. Intolerance. Segregation. Sectarian strife. Terrorism in the service of God.

Water is now rationed. Some trickles in every other day. We may use it, Homeland Dream Security has decreed, at our own risk. We can also breathe, if so compelled. The agency had the uncommon courtesy of refraining from issuing stupid directives. The old panacea -- crouch under a desk and clasp your hands over your head, seal doors and windows with duct tape and plastic sheeting -- is now the source of bitter jokes. Those who still believe in the power of prayer recite the *Pater Noster* and the 23rd Psalm. Others keep repeating, *"Eli, Eli lama sabakhtani?* God, my God, why hast thou forsaken me?"

    JEREMIAH, wheezes, looks into to camera as if into a mirror and feels the sores on his face

I lost more hair today. More teeth fell out. My gums are hemorrhaging and blood oozes from the corners of my eyes. But don't be alarmed, I feel no pain, only overpowering, unrelenting fatigue. These are "premonitory symptoms," they say. The language of disaster is so antiseptically vague. Neutron and gamma rays work slowly. But they kill in the end.

The presses stopped rolling a little after eight, on a bright, moonlit night when the second bomb exploded a mile above the city. Electromagnetic pulses triggered a massive chain reaction that silenced all communication satellites and knocked out power from coast to coast.

I spend my waking hours huddled by the radio. Short-wave transmissions are ebbing. The chatter will cease when I run out of batteries. Last I heard the snows of the Himalayas had vaporized. The mighty Amazon has run dry. Ice showers are expected over the Sahara tomorrow. Nature repays mankind's disregard for itself with justifiable contempt. Perhaps you know all that by now. *Perhaps* is such an empty word.

Pull back shot from a dying **Jeremiah**. Camera then pans toward and through the window, surveying the desolate spectacle of a New York in ruins. A bullet-riddled storefront bears graffiti reading: ***ONLY THE BRAVE DARE LET GO....*** As credits roll, Debussy's *Nocturnes* No. 3, wistful, otherworldly and eerily exultant, chimes in the background.

POSTSCRIPT

Castle Bravo (see eye in cover photo) is the code name given to one of six thermonuclear (hydrogen) bomb tests conducted by the U.S. Atomic Energy Commission in the spring of 1954 at the Eniwetok and Bikini Atolls in the Pacific. **Bravo** obliterated the small islands on which it was set off. The conflagration produced the single worst incident of fallout exposure. Scattering over 7,000 square miles of ocean and islands, it resulted in the contamination and exposure of U.S. military and civilian personnel and natives who had been moved to supposedly "safe" islands but who suffered acute radiation effects and subsequently died.

At least 200,000 people perished in Hiroshima and Nagasaki in the wake of U.S. atomic bombardments in 1945.

www.ingramcontent.com/pod-product-compliance
Lightning Source LLC
Chambersburg PA
CBHW071231260626
47162CB00004B/1518